Amazing Things Are Happening Here

.... *Stories* ....

Jacob M. Appel

Black
Lawrence
Press

Black
Lawrence
Press

www.blacklawrence.com

Executive Editor: Diane Goettel
Cover and book design: Amy Freels

Published 2019 by Black Lawrence Press.
Printed in the United States.

The stories in this volume previously appeared in the following periodicals: "Canvassing" in *Subtropics*; "Grappling" in *Southern Humanities Review*; "Embers" in *Roanoke Review*; "Helen of Sparta" in Iowa Review; "The Bigamist's Accomplice" in *Greensboro Review*; "Amazing Things Are Happening Here" in *The Ledge*; "Dyads" in *Jabberwock Review*; "Live Shells" (as "A Thanatology for Mollusks") in *Flyway*.

Amazing Things Are Happening Here

To Rosalie

Contents

· · · · · · · · · · · · · · ·

Canvassing

· · · · · · · · · · · · · · · · · · ·

I was once—briefly—a suspect in a murder investigation.

That was more than thirty years ago, during my senior year at Chalgrove Prep, and, quite frankly, it's hard to imagine the scruffy teenage romantic that I was from the vantage point of the respectable, pragmatic paterfamilias I've somehow become. When I was first appointed to the state bench, Vanessa Bonchelle's name did appear in the local papers, but only to note that I had married her younger sister. At the time of my elevation to the appellate court three years later, where I'm pleased to say I've carved out a niche for myself as an authority on criminal procedure, the media focused its attention almost exclusively on our newborn triplets, and upon Lauren's decision to have them delivered vaginally in Oslo, where her mother lives, rather than via c-section here in Rhode Island, so any mention of the Bonchelle family's tragedy was an afterthought. In fact, I might not have spoken of my teenage crush again, as Lauren and I had arrived at a tacit pact not to mention her sister, if I hadn't received an unexpected letter last month from the State Correctional Facility at Narragansett. The long, narrow envelope looked no different from the dozens of prison missives I receive at the courthouse each month—some hostile, others beseeching—yet mailed to my personal address in

Creve Coeur, to the home of my wife and daughters, it seemed an abuse. I was about to discard the envelope without opening it. Then I noticed the name printed on the back: Troy Sucram.

I stashed the letter in the pocket of my tennis shorts. My wife and I had a mixed doubles match scheduled for that Sunday morning—like I said, I've become respectable—and Lauren had dispatched me to pick up the sitter while she pumped breast milk for our baby. When I returned, my wife was still showering, so I retreated to my study and sliced open the unwelcome envelope. I feared my hands might tremble, but they remained steady. The missive itself proved concise and straightforward—written in block letters on pre-lined paper: Troy had served his full thirty years. He was set to be released at the end of the month. He intended to leave the state permanently, but wished to meet with me for a few moments before he did so.

I was still clutching the onion skin page when Lauren appeared in the doorframe, her auburn hair a luscious contrast to her pale skin and tennis whites. A lifetime of suffering had done little to dull her dazzling looks. At forty, she retained the willowy frame of a school girl—and for the first time in years, I was again struck by her similarity to the adolescent beauty I had idolized at seventeen.

"Bad news?" Lauren asked.

"Not for us," I lied, sliding the letter into a drawer. I could as easily have slid it into the wastepaper basket, but I did not. "Just another felon pleading his case."

. . . . .

Chalgrove Prep had been an all-male institution for one hundred thirty-eight venerable years before Vanessa Bonchelle and twenty-six other young women entered the academy in the autumn of 1979. To my father, a third generation alumnus, this heralded the demise of Western civilization—he referred to the girls collectively as "the camel's noses"—but those of us still in the academic trenches took the development in stride, as we had the decision to admit "working class" scholarship kids like Troy Sucram to our class six years earlier. We quickly learned new gender-neutral lyrics to "Dear Old Chalgrove" and to use the bathrooms on alternate floors. Soon enough, several of the newcomers had attached themselves to varsity lettermen; on autumn afternoons, these amorous couples leaned back-to-back in the courtyard during free periods, pushing the limits on public displays of affection. I wasn't among them. Vanessa sat directly in front of me in three of my courses—Bradford following Bonchelle alphabetically—and, during the first nine months of my junior year, we did not exchange one single word.

That's not to say that I didn't think about her constantly. Although I can't pinpoint precisely the origins of my interest in Vanessa—how her wild auburn mane and volatile idealism came to eclipse Danielle Pastarnack's delicate innocence or Sally Sewell's devil-may-care coquetry—my attraction quickly developed into a full-fledged infatuation. At that time, my experience with women was decidedly limited: I'd gone to a couple of Sadie Hawkins dances with the stepdaughter of my father's urology partner, a sweet girl who suffered from total alopecia, and had kissed her once, on her doorstep, out of curiosity and pity. Yet nothing in the first sixteen years of my life had adequately prepared me for the political whirlwind and sensual dynamo that was Vanessa Bonchelle, or for her ongoing challenge to the authorities of Chalgrove—whether that meant circulating a letter demanding that "*In deo laetandum*" be removed from the school's seal or pounding her fist on a desk while questioning Mr. Rothfeig's interpretation of the Monroe Doctrine until her breath ran out. Every detail I learned of her life rendered her that much less approachable: her mother's crown as Miss Norway and former career as the highest-paid fashion model in Europe, her father's self-made fortune in oilrig accessories and his close friendship with Prince Philip of England. Unfortunately, each day that I lacked the courage to speak to Vanessa only elevated the wall of ice between us. Once, in chemistry class, I reached forward on impulse and felt her glossy hair between my fingertips. I suspect Vanessa knew what I had done—her neck appeared to tense ever so slightly—but she didn't acknowledge my act, and I couldn't be certain. After that, even casual eye contact with Vanessa sent a shiver of mortification down my spine. I gave up hatching plots to befriend her, and instead fantasized about miracles, often farfetched or apocalyptic, that might bring us together.

Summer approached. If my miracle did not occur before the end of June, I lamented, I would have to wait until the following September for another chance at divine intervention. So I spent my weeknights studying for the SATs, and my weekend evenings shooting pool with Eddie Arcaya and Chase Flynn in Eddie's finished basement, stewing sullenly in my unspoken love. And then one muggy Saturday afternoon, our door chime rang. I expected the postman, so I answered the bell in a torn t-shirt and grass-stained sweatpants. To my amazement, Vanessa Bonchelle stood on the front porch. She sported tight acid-wash jeans and carried a clipboard. My crush appeared on the verge of speaking, but caught herself as she recognized me, and I realized that she was as shocked at the meeting as I was.

"Hey Josh," Vanessa said—as though we spoke every day. "I'm collecting signatures to place Congressman John Anderson in the Presidential ballot. Are there any registered voters at home today who would be willing to sign?"

Her lapel pin announced: MAKE THE ANDERSON DIFFER-ENCE! Humidity matted her bangs to her forehead. Before that instant, I had never heard of Congressman John Anderson, but I suddenly became his most ardent supporter.

I searched my throat for words, but found none.

A moment later, my father emerged around the side of the house. He'd been tending his rosebushes and held a pruning shears in a gloved hand. He sized up Vanessa as though appraising a prostate gland and then turned his attention to me.

"Is this a friend of yours, Joshua?" he asked.

"I don't know," I stammered.

Vanessa stepped into the breach. "I'm collecting signatures to place Congressman Anderson on the November ballot," she informed my father. "Would you be willing to sign? Signing does not mean you're agreeing to support Congressman Anderson in any way. All you'd be doing is giving voters a choice."

"I suppose you're a supporter of Anderson?" my father asked her.

"Vanessa Bonchelle," said Vanessa. "I'm the Congressman's campaign manager here in Creve Coeur." When my father did not shake her outstretched hand, she launched into a campaign salvo: "Congressman Anderson is the only major candidate who supports extending the ratification period for the Equal Rights Amendment," she began. What followed were the candidate's positions on nuclear weapons, fair housing, Amtrak. As she spoke, Vanessa's white cheeks turned crimson. I could feel my father's arteries hardening vicariously.

"I see," said my father. "Now let me tell *you* a story, young lady. When I was a surgery intern, I once worked a forty-eight hour shift in the OR. I was so tired when I finished, I pulled my car up at the stop sign outside the hospital parking lot . . . and I sat there, *waiting for the stop sign to turn green*. That's how hard *I* worked to get where I am today . . . and that's why I'm voting for Reagan."

My father snipped the air with his sheers. "You're welcome to offer your friend a snack, Joshua," he said. "Your mother left a strudel on the sideboard." And then he tossed his gloves into the stainless steel bin beside the door and vanished into the house.

"Sorry," I said.

"It's okay. I'm used to it."

An awkward silence enveloped us. The scent of crab apple blossoms wafted from the yard. Across the street, a team of laborers was repaving the Davenports' handball court, the foreman bellowing orders in Portuguese. I considered inviting Vanessa inside for a slice of apple strudel—but, at that moment, I wanted to distance myself from my father's ideas as much as possible.

"Do you need any more volunteers?" I finally asked. "I mean ... I could help you get signatures, if you wanted me to ..."

I felt the air freeze inside my lungs.

"Cool beans!" Vanessa exclaimed. "Would you like to be deputy campaign manager or press secretary?"

I had apparently doubled the size of the Anderson effort in Creve Coeur.

. . . . .

My stint with the John B. Anderson presidential campaign started the following morning when Vanessa picked me up in her flamingo-pink Chrysler Cordoba. The vehicle boasted a vinyl roof and power windows. Its owner wore white tights under a denim skirt and had a daisy pinned above her ear. A pair of his-and-hers clipboards rested on the passenger seat. Vanessa's intention was to train me in the art of collecting signatures, then to dispatch me to canvass on my own. My own goal was to glom onto her for as long as humanly possible, preferably until Anderson entered the Oval Office, in the hope that proximity would inspire romance.

"Good morning, deputy," she said. "Ready to pound the pavement?"

"Sure thing," I said.

We drove under the expressway and into the working-class Italian-and-Irish neighborhood opposite the dockyards. I had read up on Anderson the night before in back copies of *The Providence Journal* and the *Creve Coeur Clarion*—and what little I knew suggested that these ethnic Catholic tenements were unlikely to provide fertile ground to collect signatures for a liberal Republican. Nor, for that matter, were the upscale Victorians on Banker's Hill where Vanessa and I lived. Canvassing down by the college, or even at the Hutchinson Mall, made far more sense to me, but I had no intention of questioning Vanessa's tactics.

"How many signatures do we need?" I inquired.

"One thousand across the state."

"How many do we have right now?"

"As of last weekend," replied Vanessa, "we had twenty thousand four hundred."

She looked at me and beamed. "Our goal isn't really to collect signatures. That's just our cover. Our goal is to get people thinking about Anderson. But it's much easier to talk to people like your dad if you're only looking for ballot access."

"Is that official campaign strategy?" I asked.

"It is," she replied, "if I say it is."

Vanessa explained that she spoke once each week by telephone with the campaign's New England nerve center in Boston. She had no budget, no office. She'd asked for the job when she'd contacted the Anderson campaign in Washington hoping to volunteer at their Creve Coeur headquarters—and had discovered that there wasn't one. The only formal instruction she'd received was not to promise anyone an appointment in a future Anderson administration; otherwise, she was on her own. Of course, running a city-wide campaign with no budget wasn't easy. It didn't help that her father, although worth in excess of fifty million dollars, refused to spend one dime on her efforts. Victor Bonchelle made my father look like a Maoist. Eleven years later, when the entrepreneur shot himself to death—in the wake of Vanessa's murder and a series of financial setbacks—he telephoned the funeral parlor in advance to arrange the service, then laid out a dark suit on the bed for his own viewing. How a man of my late father-in-law's ilk and temperament produced a pair of free-spirited daughters remains one of life's great mysteries.

Vanessa parked at the head of a cul-de-sac and we started ringing doorbells. Some residents listened civilly and signed—although often adding, "I'm voting for Carter," even as they returned her ballpoint pen. Others offered polite excuses: they were late for church, they weren't American citizens, they did not sign petitions on principle. One elderly woman shouted at us in what sounded like Greek, shaking her raised fist. Another man barked, "I'm not voting for no colored guy," and slammed the door. I shouted back, "But Anderson's white," then realized how awful that sounded. Mostly, I let Vanessa conduct the electioneering, satisfying myself with the pleasure of hearing her impassioned voice and watching the delicate flare of his nostrils as she grew excited. My companion clung to her fierce optimism in spite of Anderson's abysmal polling numbers, constantly reminding voters that "the future is inherently unpredictable" and "anything can happen" on Election Day. *That's what makes democracy great*, she'd conclude. *That's what separates us from Moscow and Peking and Tehran.* Every so often, as we left an entryway, she'd offer me a tidbit of insight: *Don't talk about the other candidates*, she'd say. *We're canvassing, not debating.* Or: *Always fake a few signatures at the top of each page, so the voter doesn't feel that she's the first one to sign. People don't like going out on a limb.*

Around one o'clock, we bought sandwiches at a café on Drowne Boulevard and ate them on the benches in the adjacent pavilion.

Canvassing, even as a spectator, proved exhausting, and I was famished. Yet if I hoped our lunch break might provide an opportunity for more personal conversation—or even flirtation—I was to be disappointed: Vanessa spent the entire forty-five minutes comparing Anderson's national campaign with other recent political insurgents. Never have the names Morris Udall or George McGovern sounded so romantic.

We continued up Front Street that afternoon, then explored the narrow, crowded blocks between the waterfront and the train station. "It's just like when I take my baby sister trick-or-treating," said Vanessa. "You want to find the right balance between homes that are close together and people who will actually answer their bells." So while working class apartment buildings held promise, pubic housing projects generally proved a wasted effort, as many residents refused to risk opening their doors for strangers. Much of our time was spent responding to questions about Anderson's stances on issues. Here, Vanessa appeared to have an extraordinary amount of information tucked in reserve.

One cocoa-skinned man, who identified himself as "Brother André," demanded to know Anderson's position on the recent military coup in Suriname. "Is your Mr. Anderson *for* Chairman Bouterse or is he *against* Chairman Bouterse?"

"I take it you are *for* Chairman Bouterse?" said Vanessa.

Brother André scowled. "How can *any* man be *for* Chairman Bouterse? I am for freedom. Bouterse is the opposite of freedom."

"That is why Congressman Anderson was the first legislator to propose economic sanctions against the illegitimate Surinamese junta," replied Vanessa, her face suddenly aglow. And she explained, in painstaking detail, Anderson's ambitious schemes to cripple Chairman Bouterse's regime in a dozen different ways. By the end of their conversation, not only had Brother André pledged to vote for our candidate, he'd even summoned several friends from a neighboring apartment to sign Vanessa's petition. Meanwhile, I tried to recollect whether Suriname was in Africa or South America.

As we rode the elevator to the next floor, I remember thinking that a girl as beautiful and intelligent as Vanessa would *never* fall for me.

"How on earth did you know all that?" I asked her.

"All what?"

"About Chairman what's-his-name, and Congressman Anderson's attitude toward the conflict in Suriname, and all of that? Honestly, it's hard to imagine that Anderson even has an opinion on the coup in Suriname."

"He doesn't," replied Vanessa. "Not as far as I know."

"But—"

"I think fast on my feet," said Vanessa. "It doesn't matter what position the Congressman holds on any particular issue, especially an obscure one. What matters is that he'll bring good judgment and a sense of fair play to government, that he'll stand up for the underdog. I want to live in a world where people aren't judged by how much money they have, or what body they were born into, but by what they're capable of doing. If I have to bend the truth slightly to make that happen, so be it."

In hindsight, Vanessa's flexibility with the truth bordered on the sociopathic. At the time, my companion's "functional honesty"— as she termed her duplicity—rendered her all the more alluring. Yet she must have sensed my misgivings, because without warning, she paid me a compliment. "I can't tell you how happy I am that you've joined the campaign," said Vanessa. "We've only been working together for what—nine hours? And already it's hard to imagine doing this alone."

I fed off of those words for another six months.

. . . . .

I interned that summer at a neurosurgeon's office. I already knew that I had zero interest in following my Bradford forebears into medicine, but my father remained convinced that increased exposure would persuade me otherwise, so three days each week, I shadowed Dr. Moncrief, a college roommate of my great-uncle's who chain-smoked cigarettes in his examination room. What I remember most vividly of the work was that Moncrief shared a vestibule with a craniofacial surgeon named Mooney who specialized in treating severely deformed children. Thirty years later, I can still picture some of those kids—toddlers lacking ears, teenagers with deep dents in their foreheads. Eventually, I learned to enter and leave the building with my eyes closed.

On Tuesdays and Thursdays, Dr. Moncrief operated in Providence, freeing me to continue my work with the Anderson campaign. The campaign's canvassing efforts had already been scaled down to three days each week, because Vanessa's family required her presence at their Martha's Vineyard beach house over four-day weekends through the summer. My crush often complained of the flight to the island on Vincent Bonchelle's 16-seat Learjet, which terrified her, but rarely shared any details of her time away. We spoke mostly of politics—or rather, Vanessa spoke and I listened—so that, after four months of canvassing, I knew more of the private lives of Governor John Connally and Senator Howard Baker than about her own. Outside of canvassing, our social worlds existed in isolation. Vanessa didn't introduce me to her friends, mostly ex-pat girls she knew from before her arrival at Chalgrove, and I never once considered inviting her to Eddie Arcaya's basement for pool or to play ping-pong on Chase Flynn's patio.

The closest we ever came to a truly intimate conversation occurred in late June, the day Gallup released a poll that showed

Anderson surging to 26 percent nationwide. We'd stopped for ice cream at the drive-thru Friendly's. I'd just taken the SATs that Saturday, and my father had "rewarded" me with five hundred dollars in cash, so I still recall paying for a trio of fifty-cent milkshakes with a $100 bill. The third milkshake was for Vanessa to bring home to her younger sister—whom I still hadn't met.

I held Vanessa's milkshake while she drove, and periodically, my companion leaned over the gear shift for a slurp. She'd unbuttoned the top three buttons of her blouse, on account of the heat, and I had to avert my gaze to avoid her cleavage.

"What do you want to be doing in twenty years?" asked Vanessa.

Her question caught me off guard. A suave young man might have been able to say, "Spending time with you," and have pulled it off—but suave, I was not.

"I honestly don't know," I spluttered. "I haven't thought that far ahead."

Vanessa frowned—she appeared genuinely dismayed. "I'd like to be Secretary of State," she said, matter-of-fact, as though the post was hers for the asking. She adjusted the rearview mirror. "I'd also like to have six kids—three boys and three girls—and to take them traveling with me around the globe."

"Six kids is an awful lot," I replied—calibrating my own life course accordingly.

Vanessa laughed. "Sometimes I think I should have fifteen or twenty. That's the best way to leave a stamp on the electorate. They could become their own voting block."

We paused at a traffic light. Vanessa took her milkshake from my hand, her wrist brushing against my fingers.

"Do you think we'll still be friends in twenty years?" she asked.

Her choice of the word "friends" shattered my mood.

"A lot can happen in twenty years," I said.

"Not *that* much," she answered. "If two people are truly determined to stay friends, nothing should be able to stop them."

When I replied to Troy Sucram's letter, several weeks ago, I was hit with the unsettling realization that the distant future Vanessa Bonchelle looked forward to, on that sweltering summer afternoon, has already receded ten years into the past.

. . . . .

In hindsight, it's tempting to think that my time with Vanessa might have continued as it was indefinitely, if not for our encounter with Troy Sucram, but the reality was that Election Day approached rapidly. After the autumn, I'd no longer have had an excuse to explore the backstreets of Creve Coeur in Vanessa's company, and as October drifted toward November, without any romantic overtures on her part, I struggled for an opening to reframe our relationship. I considered writing Vanessa a letter to confess my feelings, or even showing up to canvass one morning armed with a dozen roses. She hadn't rejected me, after all, I assured myself; she merely hadn't yet considered me. However, I also sensed Vanessa might not be ready to consider me—and that more time together could only increase my prospects—while the artificial constraints of an election campaign threatened to force my hand. Needless to say, on the crisp, late October evening when we visited Troy, these concerns already weighed heavily upon me.

As I mentioned earlier, Troy Sucram was one of the fifteen working-class students who Chalgrove had admitted on scholarship in 1974 in order to improve the school's local image, and to stave off efforts by the municipal council to incorporate private schools into its tax base. Some of these boys—Eddie Arcaya was one of them— navigated the transition smoothly. Yet from the outset, Troy carried an enormous chip on his shoulder. He boasted—against the weight of chronological evidence—that his grandfather had been among the stonemasons who constructed Chalgrove Hall. In the library, he circled all of the vulgar words in the unabridged dictionaries. When, as part of a lesson on mass hysteria and the Salem Witch trials, our seventh grade teacher, Mr. Drapkin, reported that a dying squirrel had crawled into one of the classroom's ventilation shafts—a patent falsehood that prompted several students to complain of the dead rodent's odor—Troy actually claimed to have witnessed the creature himself. He *continued* to insist that he'd seen it, even after Mr. Drapkin revealed that the squirrel's existence had been an utter fabrication. In spite of all that, Troy had his fans, especially among the female newcomers: He was tall, and broad-shouldered, with an easy smile and a permanent five o'clock shadow that might pass for rugged.

At the end of the summer, Vanessa and I had returned to our school-year campaign schedule, canvassing evenings and weekends. Anderson had already secured a place on the November ballot, so we no longer gathered signatures. Instead, we pitched the candidate's merits directly. Vanessa now recognized that he couldn't win the general election, but she still maintained he had a shot at Rhode Island's three electoral votes. At a minimum, she wanted to win Creve Coeur. That would only be possible, she believed, if we visited every local household at least once, which is what led us to the dimly lit stretch of asphalt behind the county bus garage, where Troy Sucram's family lived in a dilapidated Cape Codder. Juniper hedges and pachysandra had entirely overrun the front walk, but at the side of the dwelling, a gate stood open in the stockade fence. The word "ENTER" had been spray-painted on the adjoining wood. A cold rain was starting to fall, slicking the path and plastering dead leaves to the slate.

Vanessa rang the bell. We heard arguing inside. Then Troy appeared in the doorframe, the portrait of nonchalance, his Boston Braves cap awry, his shirt unbuttoned and untucked.

"Whoa, whoa, whoa," Troy greeted us. "Vanessa Bonchelle in the flesh."

I stood behind Vanessa, holding open the screen door. Troy flicked me a nod of acknowledgement.

"We're campaigning for Congressman John Anderson," explained Vanessa. "He's running for President," she added. "Are your parents home?"

"Nope. But you can ask *me* for my vote."

"Are you eighteen?"

"Eighteen and four months. Getting left behind in first grade is starting to pay off," Troy said. "And I'm even registered. Surprised, aren't you?" He grinned in self-satisfaction. "Why don't you come inside and we can talk?"

I expected Vanessa to decline his invitation—she had a rule against entering homes, because it squandered too much time— but to my surprise, she let Troy Sucram lead her into his kitchen. I followed. Troy ordered his two younger brothers to "skedaddle" and cleared stacks of magazines off a pair of folding chairs for us. For himself, he transformed three milk crates into a makeshift stool. "Now why should I vote for Governor Anderson?" he asked. I sensed an energy welling in the air—emanating from both Troy and Vanessa—on a frequency entirely different from my own.

"*Congressman* Anderson," replied Vanessa. "You knew that."

"Maybe I did and maybe I didn't. . . . Anyway, what's so great about the guy?"

What ensued was the worst half hour of my life. I had heard Vanessa discuss Anderson's platform thousands of times before, but now I sensed that with each bullet point, her love was seeping through my fingers. She spoke quickly, forcefully, but she sounded uncharacteristically nervous. Troy never took his eyes off her. Meanwhile, my attention drifted from the utensils on the drainboard to the assortment of coupons and photographs affixed to the refrigerator door. I plucked a plastic ashtray off the tabletop and toyed with it mindlessly. Troy's brothers watched cartoons on a television at top volume in the next room. Rain pelted the roof. At some point, Vanessa stopped talking—her full "stump speech" ran about ten minutes—and then she waited, her back stiff and her hands folded in her lap, like a defendant expecting a verdict.

"Okay, okay," said Troy. "You make a good case."

"Thank you," answered Vanessa.

Troy's stare remained fixed on my companion. "I tell you what. If you come over here on Election Day and remind me," he said, "I'll vote for him."

Vanessa smiled playfully. "I guess I'll have to do that then."

"I guess you will."

And that was that.

Troy led us to the door and offered to lend Vanessa an umbrella. "You can return it on Election Day," he proposed. "It will give you an incentive to come back."

"No, thanks," said Vanessa. "What makes you think I need an incentive?"

"Suit yourself," he replied. "Go ahead and get wet."

Troy Sucram closed the door slowly behind us. And we did get wet. A nasty rain swept over us in sheets. Then Vanessa tugged my arm, pulling me under the overhanging eaves of the Sucram garage. The air smelled of damp plywood. Boards, some weighed down with heavy stones, lay like coffins in the nearby grass. A few of the boards had washed away, revealing mud-filled hollows. At Troy's trial, I learned these were the remnants of an abandoned horseshoe pitch.

"What was that about?" I demanded.

"You mean the umbrella?" Vanessa asked—innocently, as though nothing else unusual had transpired. "I enjoy the rain. I can handle getting wet," she said. "Besides, I don't like owing people anything."

. . . . .

When I returned home that night—toes numb, clothing soaked to the skin—I promised myself that I'd reveal my feelings to Vanessa at the next opportunity. Our plan had been to leaflet in the shopping district that weekend—the last before Election Day— with the help of volunteers from Pawtucket and Cranston. I steeled myself for my confession, but Vanessa begged off at the last moment. She had a family obligation, she claimed. So on Saturday, I manned an information booth with a sixty-something nuclear freeze activist who described Anderson as "the least of three horrific evils." On Sunday, I feigned a severe cough and avoided the business strip entirely. If Vanessa wasn't going to finish out the race, how could she blame me for bronchitis? Only afterwards did I learn that she'd spent the weekend with Troy Sucram, canvassing dorm rooms at the community college. Since I knew nothing of their rendezvous, I still hoped to profess my love. Increasingly, Election Day itself seemed like the ideal symbolic occasion. I held off contacting Vanessa on Monday, waiting for her to call, then broke down and phoned around dinnertime. "Oh, Josh! I was just thinking about you," she said—her voice instantly melting my resentment about the weekend. "Are you ready to kick some electoral college ass tomorrow?"

We agreed to meet at our local polling station at eight o'clock. Instead, ruminating in bed that night, I decided to surprise Vanessa by knocking on her door at seven. After half a year of canvassing together, I assured myself, I'd earned an hour of private dialogue. Yet I suppose I also wanted to get the matter done with—one way or another. So I tossed fitfully until daybreak, then drove the five steep blocks up Banker's Hill to the Bonchelle's Queen Anne style mansion. It was only six thirty. I waited at the curbside for twenty minutes, mustering my resolve. While I was fortifying myself, the automatic garage door opened. Seconds later, Vanessa's Cordoba backed up the drive.

The vehicle stopped at the bridge of the curb. Vanessa pulled into the street, rolling up alongside me. Chestnut liner limned her green eyes, and she looked truly radiant in the white morning light.

"Josh?" Vanessa appeared puzzled. "I thought we were meeting at eight?"

"I figured I'd surprise you," I replied. "Can I get in?"

Her expression turned anxious. She gazed out the windshield, as though seeking guidance in the muted glow of the streetlamps. I suddenly felt unwelcome, already defeated—but I knew there was no turning back.

"Do you have a few minutes to talk?" I asked again.

"I guess," she said.

I swung open the door of the Cordoba and settled into the passenger seat. Her dashboard was lacquered with fake Ronald Reagan quotations: *"I never drink coffee at lunch because I find it keeps me awake for the afternoon"* and *"It's true hard work never killed anybody, but I figure, why take the chance?"* The floor of the Cordoba was littered with donut wrappers and crushed Coke cans and empty packs of Newport cigarettes. Newport was Todd Sucram's brand— a fact made much of at trial. I found myself regretting that I hadn't penned Vanessa a love letter.

"So? What do you want to talk about?" she demanded.

"You sound upset," I said. "I thought you'd be happy to see me..."

"I have plans," she explained.

"At seven in the morning?"

"Yes, at seven in the morning. Like it's your business. I promised a handful of people I'd remind them to vote," she said. "In person."

"Okay," I said. "Why don't I come with you?"

Vanessa glanced at her watch and then back at me. Abruptly, she revved the engine into drive and we peeled away from the curbside. All of my confidence evaporated under the heat of her anger, and I found myself utterly unable to form clear thoughts, so we traversed the city in tense silence. Several times, I almost spoke—but caught myself. We'd already circled behind the county bus garage, the Cordoba's shock absorbers fighting the pock-marked pavement, when I recognized the street as Troy Sucram's. Troy's house looked different in the morning sun—even more run down than it had under cover of rain and darkness. A rusted tricycle protruded from the pachysandra, displaying the stump of an amputated rear wheel. Dogs yelped angrily behind a neighbor's chain-link fence. Vanessa pulled the Cordoba into Troy's driveway.

"So *these* are the couple of voters?" I snapped.

"Good God! What is wrong with you?"

"What is wrong *with me*? I spend six months working with you and now you don't even have the time to talk for five minutes?"

"All right, talk," said Vanessa. "Nobody's stopping you."

I took a deep breath. I hadn't planned to share my feelings while parked outside a rival's house, but I had few options. "What I was hoping to say," I finally said, "was that I think you're the most amazing person in the world." I felt like a man clinging to a ledge, my body simmering with adrenaline and desperation. "I guess what I'm saying," I continued, "is that I'm falling in love with you..."

I had much more to share, but I didn't have an opportunity.

"Please don't," interjected Vanessa. "Oh, Josh. I was afraid of this. Everybody warned me, but I didn't listen."

"Give me a chance," I said—sensing the ground had crumbled beneath me. "Do you know how you're always saying that you want to live in a world where people aren't judged by what body they were born into, that you want to stand up for the underdog? Well, this is your chance. *I am the underdog.*"

"I can't," replied Vanessa.

"Whatever. You mean you *won't.*"

"I need to go meet Troy now. I'm already late," she said. She opened the car door. "I'm so sorry, Josh. Honestly, I am."

I followed her through the wooden gate. In the Sucrams' backyard, the uncovered mud pits created an ominous moonscape. I cut diagonally across the sea of the stones and plywood, blocking Vanessa's path to the house.

"You're a fraud!" I shouted. "Do you really think I give a damn about John Anderson? There is no fucking Anderson difference! You're all the same."

Vanessa remained calm and impassive—and that only added to my fury. "I don't have time for this right now, Josh," she said. "Please get out of my way." She stepped off the path into the mud, turning her back on me. I still remember the sun glistening off her silky auburn hair, so close a person could reach out and touch it.

· · · · ·

Troy Sucram was released from prison on Monday morning, and on Tuesday afternoon, he rang my doorbell at the appointed hour. I'd agreed to meet him at home in Creve Coeur, fearing a visit to my chambers might draw notice. Fortunately, the triplets have ballet lessons after school on Tuesdays, so Lauren drives them out to Providence, the baby in tow, and my brood makes a "girls' day" of it, leaving me king of my castle until suppertime. I saw no point in telling Lauren about Troy. She'd only been nine years old when they found her sister's body—facedown under a plywood board in Troy Sucram's yard—but even the mention of his name is enough to retraumatize her.

I'd remembered Troy as tall and lean, but the man who arrived at my house weighed northwards of three hundred pounds. "That's the psych meds," he explained, sitting opposite me in my study. "Once they start pumping that shit into you, Josh, they never stop." He sipped his coffee. "Good coffee," he said, licking his lips. "They gave me meds to take with me, but the first thing I did was toss them into a sewer."

I was accustomed to people like Troy Sucram addressing me as "Judge" or "Your Honor," so his use my first name unsettled me. He had every right to, of course—this was technically a social visit—but I didn't have to like it.

At first, Troy spoke only of himself: of prison life, of his future plans. "Not much a fellow can do after thirty years away," he said, "but I'm going to try." His youngest brother ran a motel in some southern state—Alabama or Arkansas—and he'd offered Troy a job and a place to stay. "I'm a hell of a lot luckier than most guys," observed Troy. "Most guys start with absolutely nothing." He rested his hands on his enormous paunch, as though he'd just gorged himself on a feast.

"I'm glad to hear that things are looking up for you," I said—in the tone I usually reserve for the bench. "I sincerely hope you're able to turn things around."

"Thanks," said Troy. "I mean, really. Thanks."

My guest flashed a smile and I saw that he had no upper teeth. It staggered me that the man seated across from me was only forty-eight, a year older than I was, although he truly appeared closer to seventy. Gone were his rugged good looks and the insouciant charm that had beguiled journalists during his trial. If anything, thirty years in Narragansett had rendered Troy Sucram likable—the sort of person who, under very different circumstances, I might enjoy meeting for dinner.

"Is there something *I* can do for you, Troy?" I asked. "I confess I'm not entirely sure why you wanted to see me . . ."

"I'm not entirely sure either," replied Troy. "I did *not* come here to tell you that I didn't do it. *That* I'm sure of. I've had that argument far too many times—even with myself, when I hit bottom—and it's a train that left the station years ago." My guest poured a second packet of artificial sweetener into his coffee; when he spoke, he addressed his coffee cup as much as he did me. "I suppose I thought that speaking to you might reveal something. Anything. Maybe I wanted you to tell me that Vanessa *did* meet you at your polling place at eight o'clock that morning, that you *did* campaign with her that afternoon—that everything since has been the fantasy." Troy rubbed his face with his swollen hands, as though waking up from a deep slumber. "I suppose that, after all these years, I hoped something might finally make sense."

"She *didn't* show up that morning," I said. "I wish she had."

I had campaigned the entire day—nursing my sore feet from the long hike across town, careful not to encroach within twenty yards of the voting booths—and then I returned home to watch the election returns on television. One by one, Walter Cronkite called states for Carter and Reagan. Congressman Anderson drew 14 percent of the vote in Rhode Island, but most of those ballots came from Providence or near the state university; in Creve Coeur, he barely broke 10 percent. As I watched, I was struck by how organized and inherently predictable the process appeared. Vanessa had been wrong: anything *couldn't* happen. The system is designed to favor certain outcomes, a truth I now finding comforting; few disruptions are strong enough to alter its course. Later that week, when the police retraced my footsteps, hundreds of voters recalled speaking with me outside the polling station. I've often wondered how Troy Sucram spent his final days of freedom, in that short interval before suspicion shifted from me to him.

Troy Sucram stood up and shook my hand.

"I suppose some things *never* make sense," he said.

"I suppose they don't," I agreed.

We shook hands in the foyer—for what presumably would be the last time—and then Troy Sucram gave me a brief and unexpected hug. In that moment, his embrace felt so sincere, so human, that it was possible to forget that both of us had once loved the same teenage beauty, and that one of us had killed her, and for a few fleeting seconds, even I wasn't certain which one of us had crushed her skull with the stone.

Grappling
· · · · · · · · · · · · · · · ·

Arthur Dobbins first heard the story of the alligator rodeo in
1924. He was sitting at the bar in the dining room of the Cormorant Island Lodge, drinking an illegal scotch and soda. Several
other men were loafing at the bar—the ferry captain, one of the
brothers who owned the island's pepper plantation, a citrus buyer
from Ft. Coleman—and they took turns interrupting the grizzled
bartender as he spun his favorite yarn. The air was thick with cigar
smoke. Overhead, the ceiling fans buzzed like giant moths.

"Eight years ago if it's a day," said Earl, the bartender. "Nineteen
hundred and sixteen. Back when Wilson was still keeping us out
of the war."

It was a tale the men knew like their own hats, but it lost nothing with the retelling.

· · · · ·

Oriana Bingham had been eleven years old in 1916, the year
the lodge hosted its first and only New Year's Day alligator rodeo.
Her father, Commodore Langtree Bingham, had already turned a
fortune on the old hotel and now hoped to leave his cultural mark
on the state. He spared no expense. A team of black men from the
mainland had been hired to construct a horseshoe-shaped grand-

stand around the wrestling pits, and a retired auctioneer from the sugar exchange up in Tampa had been brought in to act as master of ceremonies. Stalls of slash pine were constructed for the most distinguished spectators, shaded enclosures on stilts that strived to imitate the opera boxes of New York and Paris. Among the distinguished guests at the Cormorant Island Lodge that afternoon were Florence Lawrence, Thomas Edison, and General Pershing.

Commodore Langtree sat front row center. He was flanked by his daughter, a dreamy wisp of a child in a white summer dress, and by his Yankee wife, a delicate pink-faced woman who'd never adjusted to passing the Christmas season in a warm climate. Adelaide Bingham worried aloud that she might contract malaria or that the grandstand might collapse or that one of the oversized lizards might climb from the foggy water and carry off her girl. But the band struck up a chorus of *Shine On, Harvest Moon* and everything fell into place without a hitch. Two black servants baited the animals with chunks of tarpon meat and taunted them with a wire cage of young gators. The babies yelped *y-eonk, y-eonk, y-eonk*; the adults hissed anger through their nostrils. Next, each of the grapplers was given his chance to try a hand at bulldogging, the perilous and elusive art of wrestling shut the gator's jaw and holding it closed between one's neck and one's chin. No easy feat with the reptiles straining their thick muscular tails in an effort to shake the competitors loose. One by one the contenders stepped forward: men missing fingers, men with jagged scars across their chests. One by one they failed. Only a previously unknown grappler named Jeb Moran managed to clasp shut the jaws of the largest bull gator for the requisite thirty seconds. This Moran was a scrappy matchbox of a man who competed shirtless and barefoot. When Bingham stood on the podium and awarded him the first prize bounty, the grappler counted his cash in front of the spectators.

The two men were posing for photographs, the old hotelier grinning, the young grappler staring defiantly beyond the camera, when one of the bull gators snapped his jaw shut around Oriana's exposed foot. The gator thrashed his head wildly, rolling back and forth until he'd drawn the girl's face under the water. Silence lapped across the crowd as the onlookers realized what had happened. Commodore Langtree charged down to the edge of the swamp where his wife, screeching like a wounded cat, struggled against the restraint of two burly grapplers. The other contenders stood helpless at the edge of the pit. They had been required to check their firearms up at the hotel, and only a crazy man would throw himself between a bull gator and his prey. But then Jeb Moran was in the water, his legs wrapped around the scoot of the lizard's back. He rode the beast hysterically, almost sexually. Its teeth remained clamped to bone, its body thrashing against the weight of its assailant. Moran responded by digging his thumbs deep into the gator's eyes, so deep he touched skull, so deep brain flecked his wrists, his chest, so deep the animal's pain seemed like his own.

A surgeon at the army hospital removed what remained of Oriana's foot. When she awoke from the chloroform, somehow still wearing a blooming smile, she'd immediately asked after Jeb Moran. But he was long gone.

· · · · ·

The bartender grinned at Dobbins with the satisfaction of a man who has only one good story to tell, but knows that he tells it well. He tossed a quarter into the air and caught it with is other hand. "The old commodore even offered a reward," he said. "Five thousand dollars in cash. But we never heard heads nor tails of the fellow again."

"He didn't put the money up at first," said the ferry captain. He was a tall man with military shoulders and as face as impassive as a clam shell. "She wouldn't give him no peace."

"Right you are," agreed the bartender. "Morning, noon and night that girl went after the old commodore about tracking down Moran. Said she was gonna marry him and all. Child's talk. You and I both know the daughters of men like Commodore Langtree don't marry gator grapplers. But then the old missus died and the girl was a grown woman and still she was saying she wanted Moran."

The citrus buyer dabbed his forehead with a handkerchief. "Malaria," he said.

"The old missus died of malaria," explained the bartender. "That's pushing four years ago, if it's been a Sunday. That near broke the old commodore. It's the girl that keeps him going. He dotes on her like she was the first child ever born."

The pepper grower laughed bitterly. "Lord knows why," he said. "She doesn't give a lick for the old bastard. She'd sell this place right out from under him, if she could, and move off to Jacksonville or New York City or wherever."

The bartender waved his dishrag at the pepper grower. "Love gone sour."

"Arrogant bitch," muttered the pepper grower.

"You'd be singing a different song if it was you she was after," said the bartender. He topped off all of the glasses along the bar. "The thing is, Dobbins—you don't mind me calling you Dobbins, do you?—she's turned down half the men in Pelican Bay and Ft. Coleman. She's stuck on a pipedream, if you ask me."

"But they don't ask you, Earl, do they?" said the pepper grower.

All four men laughed heartily. Dobbins smiled.

"And you say this Moran never showed up?" he asked.

The pepper grower looked at his wristwatch. "Not yet. But it's only noon."

The other loafers liked that; they laughed hard. The citrus grower slapped his knee to express his pleasure.

"I take it these suitors are after the inheritance," said Arthur Dobbins. "If this Moran fellow won't have her for five thousand dollars, she can't be much to look at."

Dobbins had been something of a wit at the agricultural college, and on the dinner circuit in Jacksonville, and he'd expected his joke to go over well. It didn't. The citrus buyer coughed and shifted his weight uncomfortably. The ferry captain and the pepper grower stared at Dobbins like slabs of petrified wood. Earl wiped down the bar and then scrubbed vigorously at a minor stain. She'd already leaned her wooden crutch against the counter when Dobbins caught her reflection in the wall mirror.

"Good morning, Miss Oriana," said the bartender.

The ferry captain tipped his cap. "Morning, ma'am," he said.

Oriana Bingham smiled at the men. The old commodore's daughter was a petite girl with gentle features and long dark hair than flowed down to her waist. She might have been thought merely pretty, in the ordinary way, if not for a set of sharp black eyes that ignited her entire visage with a tormented and passionate beauty. A wicker basket of freshly cut lilacs dangled from her arm, and now she tucked one of the flowers into an empty vase by the window. Arthur Dobbins fingered the camellia blossom in his lapel. He felt vaguely inadequate and, for the first time in his memory, at a loss for words.

"We were just saying…" said Dobbins.

"I heard what you were saying, sir," answered Oriana. She made her way around the room, refreshing the bouquets on the dining tables. Her wooden foot thumped against the parquet floor, but even without her crutch, she was surprisingly agile. Dobbins thought she might say something more, but she didn't.

"I do beg your pardon," said Dobbins. "It was a stupid thing to say."

"Yes, it was," said Oriana.

She asked the bartender for a glass of ice water and then carried her drink to a shaded alcove beside the gramophone box. At first, Dobbins thought this might be an invitation for him to join her in a secluded spot, but the girl quickly immersed herself in novel.

"I say," said Dobbins. "I'm the new naturalist."

He was fresh off his master's degree in zoology—or almost fresh. He'd been enjoying the easy life on the East Coast for several months, but tired quickly of Jacksonville's provincial notions of high society. Commodore Langtree had hired him sight unseen to lead guided wildlife tours for the guests.

"My specialty is herpetology," he added. "Turtles, gators."

Oriana looked up sharply; she closed the book around her fingers to hold her place.

"Look, I'm sorry," said Dobbins. "Let's be friends. My name's Arthur. We *have* to be friends, Miss Bingham, because I've already determined to like you."

The girl rose and advanced toward the French doors. "I know who you are, Mr. Dobbins," said Oriana. "And I *don't* like you."

"Not yet. But that will change. You'll get to know me better."

"I doubt it," answered Oriana. "I stick to my snap judgments."

. . . . .

The dapper young naturalist wasn't accustomed to rejection. His life, prior to his arrival on Cormorant Island, had been one of self-satisfied ease. From his father, he'd received the proceeds of a lucrative drygoods business and from his mother he'd acquired the delicate good looks that make women think a man sensitive and poetic. Both parents had also possessed the good sense to die young, leaving him ample opportunity to use of his inheritance. He had studied zoology to take part in the rich intellectual life of

the state agricultural college at Lake City and had come to the
lodge to enjoy the company of the wealthy and famous. Nobody
could have been more surprised than Arthur Dobbins himself
when what started off as the challenge of winning Oriana Bingham's affections degenerated into full-fledged love.

Dobbins pressed his suit on all occasions, trying to make himself useful. On hot afternoons, when Oriana read in the garden,
he insisted on bringing her pitchers of iced lemonade; during cool
evenings, when she rocked on the porch swing, he appeared at her
side with a shawl. She had to express only the most idle desire for
any object, a motion picture projector, a fresh peach out of season,
and the naturalist delivered it to her door. Once he even went to
far as to copy several sonnets from a volume in the library and
present them to her on one knee. All of these maneuvers made the
young naturalist the talk of the hotel bar, where odds were running two-to-one against him, but they did nothing to win the girl's
heart. Nor did Commodore Langtree's blessing help. One evening
at supper, Oriana's father, himself a graduate of Annapolis, class of
eighty-seven, had declared that he'd always wanted a college man
for a son-in-law, and that he deeply wished his daughter would
make a match before he passed on. She responded by urging the
old commodore to live a long life.

A full year passed. Slowly Dobbins lost his *joie de vivre*. He sat for
hours on the rotting grandstand beside the swamp, contemplat-
ing, trying to get the girl out from under his skin. Often he dozed
off and woke shivering in a dew-drenched shirt. The naturalist
could still be counted on for a good jest in the drawing room and
a honed quip at the bar, but now his clothes hung a bit looser from
his already thin frame, and his eyes wandered during conversation, and sometimes, while leading a tour at dusk along the wind-
swept beach or listening to a sad song on the gramophone, his eyes

moistened with longing. Nearly every night he asked Oriana if she wished to accompany him on an outing the following morning, a picnic at Lighthouse Point, a fishing excursion into Great Tarpon Sound. Nearly every night she rejected him, sometimes turning away without a word. And then she changed her mind. Without warning. One perfectly ordinary evening, he walked her to the foot of the stairs and invited her on a canoe trip through the mangroves. At first she walked away. But when she reached the top of the staircase, she turned and said, "Yes, Mr. Dobbins, a canoe trip. I think that would be a good idea."

. . . . .

They were out on the water shortly after daybreak. The naturalist had suffered a hell of a time scrounging up a canoe at the last minute—he'd actually had to purchase the boat from a black shrimper—but he had no regrets. He was alone in the wilderness with Oriana Bingham, her small round shoulders only an oar-length away. What more could a man ask for? Dobbins drove the paddle with long deep strokes and the vessel responded with the graceful glide of an anhinga.

Dobbins was afraid to speak. He didn't want to jeopardize the moment. He finally said, "It's hard to believe you've come around. I was beginning to fear you were stubborn enough to hold out on principle."

Oriana didn't answer. They turned into a narrow channel where a pair of night herons huddled on the leeward shore. A long log sat like a gator in the water.

"I'm so happy," said the naturalist, "I'm trembling. Look at me. My hands are shaking."

Oriana turned her head back toward him. She wasn't smiling. "I'm sorry, Mr. Dobbins... Arthur... but I'm afraid I've given you the wrong impression. I came out with you today to make it clear once and for all that your persistence will get you nowhere."

Dobbins pulled the paddle into the boat. "Jesus Christ," he said.

"I was wrong about you," said Oriana. "I said I wasn't going to like you and the truth is that I *have* grown to like you. I really have. You're kind, and considerate, and sometimes you can be downright funny. Only I'm not going to like you *in that manner*. The way a wife loves a husband. But if you drop your silly courtship, Arthur, I do think we could be friends."

"Friends," echoed Dobbins. His heartbeat accelerated like an avalanche. "But if you were wrong about not liking me, how do you know you won't be wrong about not loving me?"

Oriana sighed. "A woman knows these things." She took a sip of water from her canteen. "Let's try to have a good time today," she said. "Why don't we talk about something else for a change?"

"Like what?"

"Like Jacksonville," said Oriana. "What was it like?"

"It's a city. There's not much to say about it. I'm much happier out here where you don't have to worry about getting run over by motorcars."

"I'd rather get hit by a motorcar than waste away in the middle of nowhere," said Oriana. "I don't really mean that. But sometimes I get so tired."

"Of taking care of Commodore Langtree?"

"Oh I don't know," she said. "Of everything."

Dobbins spotted a bull gator sunning himself on the opposite bank. He recalled a conversation he'd once had with a fellow herpetologist at the agricultural college. The graduate student, a woman, had asked him whether he thought reptiles fell in love. He'd said yes, at least alligators did. You could see the lust in their eyes.

"Is it because you don't find me physically attractive?" asked Dobbins. He'd never experienced this before, but it was possible.

"Please, Arthur," Oriana answered sharply.

"I have a right to know why."

She nodded. "I guess you do," she said in a softer voice. "Only I don't know if I can explain. I feel like I waited all my childhood for someone to rescue me. A girl dreams that a man will put his life on the line for her. Most girls only dream, of course. But in my case someone actually did."

The canoe lurched suddenly. Dobbins flailed at the air with his paddle as the vessel rose several feet above the water and landed upright with a splash. A six-foot-long shadow coasted across the channel like a giant gray potato.

"It's a manatee," explained the naturalist. "Isn't she beautiful?"

Oriana shook the water from her hair. "I'd rather see Jacksonville."

This made Dobbins angry. He couldn't count the times he'd offered to take her away from the island. "Jeb Moran's not coming back," he said. "Why can't you get that through your thick skull and move on with your life?"

"Take me home," she answered. "Now."

The naturalist considered paddling out toward the manatee and staging a second accident on their return voyage. If she wanted to be rescued, he thought, he'd show her rescue. Then he considered the risks. She might drown. They both might drown. The manatee might knock him unconscious. But it was the gators that scared him most: He couldn't afford to hobble through life with a wooden crutch and a matching wooden foot. At first, Dobbins steered toward the open water, measuring his courage with each stroke, but at the last moment he cut back toward the shallows and followed the trail to the lodge.

. . . . .

Dobbins didn't have much time to adjust to his formal rebuff. Two weeks later, like spit in his eye, Jeb Moran sauntered into the dining room of the hotel. The grappler had stripped down to a white undershirt, and the sinews were visible in his lean, muscular arms. He'd picked up a tattoo of a dagger on his left biceps; he'd also lost the tip of his nose. Still there was no mistaking the wrestler with his rough-hewn features and angry brow.

"Well dog my cats," exclaimed the bartender. "You're Jeb Moran."

The grappler set his carpet bag on the floor. He grinned. "Yeah, I'm Jeb Moran."

Conversation died out at the bar. The citrus buyer grudgingly removed a crisp twenty-dollar bill from his wallet and handed it to the pepper grower. Arthur Dobbins felt the heat creeping up his neck like a rash.

"Where's Bingham?" asked Moran. "He owes me money."

The bartender slid a whiskey in front of Moran. "So you're going to marry her?"

"For five thousand dollars," said the grappler. "Where's Bingham?"

"Take a load off," said the bartender. "The doc's in with Commodore Langtree right now. They'll be done soon. You waited this long, surely you can wait half an hour."

"Bingham sick?" asked Moran.

The citrus buyer slapped his hand against his chest. "Ticker," he said.

Moran nodded. He polished off the whiskey and smacked the shot glass down on the counter. The bartender filled him up.

"So where you been all this time?" asked the pepper grower.

Moran cut him a sidelong glance. "I fought in the war."

This drew a murmur of approval; two fisherman drank to the war.

Arthur Dobbins asked, "On which side?"

The citrus buyer chuckled nervously. Moran squared his shoulders. "What was that?"

"Nothing," said Dobbins. "But the war's been over some time now. Maybe it took you six years to muster out."

Several of the men at the bar laughed aloud; they cleared a circle around the naturalist and the grappler.

"I spent some time up near Gainesville," said Moran. "What's it to you?"

"Gainesville," answered Dobbins. "You've been studying at the women's college, have you?"

More laughter. The pepper grower chortled his drink through his nose.

"I been up at Raiford," said Moran. "The state pen."

"What happened? Did they catch you cheating at the women's college? Or did they find out which side you fought on in the war?"

Moran rubbed the nub of his missing nose. "A fellow tried to cheat me out of my bounty, so I threw him in the gator pit." The grappler drew a knife from his belt and twirled the point on the bar. "Don't fool with me, okay? I'm aiming not to get sent back up."

Commodore Langtree's voice answered from the doorway. "Who's getting sent where?"

The hotelier lumbered into the dining hall and rested both his hands on his dragon-headed walking stick. His eyes shifted from Moran to Dobbins to Moran. He appeared about to speak when his daughter and the plump physician passed through the French doors in heated conversation. The girl recognized Moran. She stopped speaking mid-sentence.

Moran stepped toward the old Commodore. "I done come for a wife."

Oriana didn't give her father the chance to answer. She dragged her foot quickly across the dining hall and Dobbins could only watch as she kissed the ligaments of the grappler's neck and the hollows of his eyes and thin gray lips that reluctantly kissed her back.

· · · · ·

The Methodist minister from Pelican Bay performed the service on the site of the alligator rodeo. There was no master of ceremonies, no band. Jeb Moran wore one of Commodore Langtree's white summer suits whose sleeves hung down to the tips of his fingers. The young couple experienced a fleeting interval of happiness during which Oriana hung onto her husband's elbow while the grappler counted out the reward money dollar for dollar. The sun stamped the sky like a newly-minted coin. Gators drifted across the wrestling pits. The old Commodore stood posing for photographs at the base of the grandstand when the structure wheezed deeply, like a child with the croup, and toppled forward in a dam break of slash pine. Bingham's skull was crushed instantly. Jeb Moran was now married to the owner of the Cormorant Island Lodge and the employer of Arthur Dobbins.

· · · · ·

Married life did little to improve the ways of the grappler. He presented himself in the dining hall during the supper hour wearing only his bathing trunks and swigged whiskey straight from the bottle. Sometimes he sat down uninvited at a guest's table. On other occasions—if he were drunk enough—he urinated on the floor behind the bar. But most of his time was spent wrestling alligators, either alone in the swamp behind the lodge or in shanty towns up and down the coast. These trips took him away for days at a time. Once in a while, he returned with a bandaged wound, but more often he arrived home gloating over his bounty. He also took an interest in cock fighting and shooting dice with the black men who worked in the hotel kitchen. "When you're raised poor enough," he said, "you learn there's no crime winning money off niggers." Moran might have been the richest man in the county, through his wife's property, but he resisted almost by instinct all the trappings of that role.

The only time Moran expressed concern for Commodore Bingham's fortune was when he suspected that his bride was trying to cheat him out of it. Most often this occurred when he returned home from the mainland without a bounty. He drank himself angry and let the accusations flow. Nobody was immune. Not the two brothers who owned the pepper plantation. Not the overweight physician. Not Earl behind the bar. Moran grilled his suspect for several hours at a stretch—the regulars knew enough to humor him with their denials—and railed at Oriana for the remainder of the night. The couple's rows kept the whole hotel awake. But they were sporadic, maybe once a month, and comical enough, in light of the farfetched conspiracies imagined by the grappler, that some of the regulars made a game of sitting up in the lobby to eavesdrop. Whoever was the subject of the night's deranged charges drank for free while the others paid tribute to his alleged cunning and his sexual prowess.

Oriana accepted her husband's moods. She bore his insults and his curses until he passed out, then pulled off his heavy boots and washed the mud from his body with a sponge. Once he hit her so her eye swelled shut. Another time, he fractured her arm. She always appeared in the lobby the next morning with her head high and a determined smile on her face. If ever the girl second-guessed her marriage, she kept her regrets under lock and key.

Arthur Dobbins' feelings were another matter. He'd never much understood the desires and motives of others, especially women, and Oriana Moran's attachment to her husband struck him as both perverse and spiteful. It might have been different if the grappler treated her right, if they'd visited Niagara Falls and New York City, but Moran had nixed the idea of a honeymoon. "If you want to see nigger policemen," he'd said, "go yourself." The naturalist couldn't figure why a girl who'd only months before spoken longingly of moving to the big city would be willing to spend forever on a backwater barrier island. I have everything to offer her, thought Dobbins. He doesn't even have a goddam nose. The young naturalist wandered the sycamore barrens, growing angrier by the day. He didn't understand what he'd done wrong.

· · · · ·

One chilly January night Moran wandered into the lodge worse off than usual. His sleeves were caked in mud to the elbows and a stripe of dried blood ran diagonally like a sash across his shirt. More blood dripped from a gash that sliced his cheek to the ear. The annual Robert E. Lee Day dinner dance was winding down when the grappler entered the dining hall, and the Ft. Coleman orchestra had just taken up a reprise of *It Had to Be You.*

The grappler found Dobbins sitting backwards on the bar, his feet resting gingerly on a barstool. The naturalist was telling a story to three women in their twenties, the daughters of a midwestern real estate speculator who'd come down to Cormorant Island for the winter. Usually Moran—even on a bender—left Dobbins alone. But it so happened that the naturalist's story, sentimental and self-pitying, was about a hotelier's daughter who spurns a handsome gentleman for a disfigured ne'er-do-well. This was too much for the drunken grappler.

Moran pushed his way between the ladies. "Where'd you sleep last night?"

Dobbins folded his spectacles into his pocket. "You're drunk, Moran," he said.

"Don't tell me what I am," said Moran. He wiped his wound with his arm, spreading mud across his face. "Where the hell d'ya sleep?"

The bleeding grappler started to draw attention. Oriana had already gone to bed, but the bartender sent one of the black youths to rouse her. Another servant was sent down the road for the plump physician.

"I asked you something," said Moran. "Where the hell d'ya sleep?"

There was nothing new in the question. Moran had, at one time or another, asked the same of half the men in the room. They had sworn their alibis in good humor. They expected the naturalist to do the same. Dobbins merely smiled as though he'd been looking forward to the grappler's harangue. "You want to know where I slept?" he asked. "I'll tell you. I slept in a bed."

"So you're gonna be a wiseacre," said Moran. "*Whose* bed?"

Dobbins shrugged. "It's hard to remember."

"I'll tell you where you slept," Moran shouted back. "You slept in *my* bed. I've been on to you all along, how you and that bitch have been plotting to sell this place out from under me. You think just because I don't got a fancy carnation in my lapel, I don't know which end is up."

"Mrs. Moran and I?" asked Dobbins, grinning. "Why would you think that?"

"So you're denying it?" demanded Moran.

The naturalist said nothing. Several of the regulars answered for him, assuring Moran that his accusations were off-base. The band continued to play to an empty dance floor.

"I'll give you one last chance," said Moran. "Are you plotting with my wife?"

"Tell him the truth," urged the bartender. "C'mon, Dobbins."

Dobbins leaned toward Moran. "The truth?" he said in a sopping-sweet voice that oozed with insincerity. "The truth is that Mrs. Moran is madly in love with her husband."

Moran reached for his knife and discovered the sheath was empty. Several onlookers tried to restrain him, but he shook them off. He swaggered toward the lobby and when he reached the foot of the stairs he shouted, "Coward!"

. . . . .

That night the naturalist dreamed that he and Moran were wrestling, that the grappler held him half-submerged in the alligator pit and was gutting him, in and out, with a knife. When he woke the sun was streaming through the open window and someone was beating on the door. "Coming," Dobbins called. "Hold your damn horses." He poured himself a shot of scotch to scrape the cat hair from his tongue and then slipped on his robe.

"Please Arthur! Open up!"

He drew the bolt. Oriana tumbled into the bedroom. Her hair was bunned under a mesh bonnet and she was holding her dressing gown closed with her hand.

"What did you do to him?" she cried.

Dobbins helped her into a chair. "Are you okay?"

"You have to stop him," said Oriana. "He has this crazy idea that we're plotting against him, that we're in cahoots behind his back. He says you said so."

"I told him just the opposite," Dobbins answered calmly. "Did he threaten you?"

"He said he's leaving. He packed all his things. You have to stop him Arthur. Please tell him it's all in his head."

"What good will that do? I already told him."

Oriana broke into sobs. Dobbins grew aware that his room was a mess, that the water pitcher was overturned and the bedding was jumbled on the floor. He vaguely recalled Earl and the physician carrying him up the stairs.

"There, there," soothed Dobbins. He offered her a glass of scotch and she drank.

"Please, Arthur," begged Oriana. "I don't know what I'll do if he leaves. I swear it will kill me. . . . If you ever cared for me at all . . ."

Dobbins hadn't expected this. "Where is he?"

"He's down by the swamp, saying goodbye," said Oriana. "I'll show you."

. . . . .

They found Moran squatting on the plywood jetty that bisected the wrestling pits. Between his knees sat an iron bucket from which he tossed chunks of fish to the gators. The grappler's carpet bag rested on the nearby sand. Dobbins shivered against the nip in the air.

"Jeb, dear," said Oriana. "Mr. Dobbins wants to speak with you." She hobbled onto the pier and placed her palm on her husband's shoulder. He jolted.

"Mind your business," said Moran.

The naturalist stood at the base of the jetty. "Look, Moran," he said. "I'm afraid I might have given you the wrong impression that night. If I said anything to make you think—well, I just don't think you have cause to run off."

Moran stood up and kicked the empty bucket into the water. The entire left side of his face was wrapped in gauze. "Lying coward," he muttered.

"I'm not lying now," said Dobbins.

"Please, Jeb," pleaded Oriana. "Please listen."

"I heard all I need to hear."

Moran stepped forward and Oriana grabbed his arm. "I love you."

"Well, I don't love you," he snapped. The grappler swallowed several times and then spit into the swamp. "I'm fucking done with this."

"Hold on a second," said Dobbins.

"You want her so bad?" shouted Moran. "You can have her."

The grappler lifted his wife up suddenly and tossed her sideways into the water. She landed with a broad splash about ten feet out and her body actually clipped the tail of a gator. Moran grinned. "She's all yours, coward. Go get her."

Arthur Dobbins stood frozen on the shoreline. He suddenly remembered the story of the alligator rodeo and how Moran had fought the animal by gouging out its eyes. That was what the occasion demanded. He would jump in the water and use his thumbs as knives. He would do it. He *would*. These were his thoughts as Oriana's body vanished into the depths.

· · · · ·

This all took place a lifetime ago. Jeb Moran hopped the next ferry and vanished forever into the wild expanse of mainland America. Some say he was killed in a knife fight up in Okaleechee and others that he drowned smuggling small arms into Cuba, but it would be pleasant to imagine he died grappling with gators, which, after all, was the only thing he'd ever been any good it. Arthur Dobbins also quit Cormorant Island. He opened a popular seafood restaurant in Ft. Coleman, married a cousin of Anne Morrow Lindbergh, and died of renal failure at the age of forty-seven. The century hurricane of 1951 swept Commodore Langtree's lodge into the gulf. All that remains of Old Florida are the memories of women like Oriana Moran. She is well past ninety and doesn't recall much. What she does remember is the morning her heart shattered, and the long cold sleep of death, and then the humiliation of waking up in the arms of a man she could never love. "You rescued me," she'd said with her first dry breath. "I wanted to drown."

Embers

· · · · · · · · · · · ·

Through the hormone-frenzied expanse of adolescence, my fantasy life revolved around a saffron-haired beauty named Vanessa Vidalgo. She'd entered our class in eighth grade, the same year Larry DeGraw was paralyzed in a skiing accident and "Patty" Finn returned as "Tricia" from her bicycle tour of Australia. Vanessa's father was a fireman—a rarity in our commuter suburb, where most parents were white-collar professionals or stay-at-home moms—but when Amity Cove's rough-edged fire chief suffered a massive coronary responding to a false alarm, the Board of Selectmen brought in well-spoken, college-educated Al Vidalgo, a deputy fire commissioner from Boston, to replace him. The town rented his family a three-bedroom colonial on Saratoga Street to sweeten the deal. I've picked up these details from my mother, who was First Selectman at the time, the equivalent of part-time mayor, but what interested me then were the perilously-high hemlines of Vanessa's denim skirts and the bulge of her well-developed chest against her angora sweaters. Yet when the Vidalgos visited our house for a welcome reception that August, and my mother introduced us, I responded to Vanessa's friendly smile with a sheepish grin—and retreated into our kitchen. After that, we shared a schedule of "honors" classes for an entire school year, but managed not to exchange a single word. The fault was mine. If she glanced in my direction, I looked away, petrified that she'd detect my desire. But I squandered whole afternoons dreaming up scenarios—from hostage crises to smallpox quarantines—that might force us together.

I was far from alone in my feelings. My best friend, Marty Kleetz, crowed his passion shamelessly. When I turned fifteen, and acquired my driving permit, Marty insisted that we cruise Saratoga Street each afternoon on the way home from archery practice, so that he could inspect the cars parked outside Vanessa's home. Other guys, older, more popular, took her to lacrosse matches, to concerts at McConkey's Arena, probably to fool around in the nature preserve behind the public library. They moved in social orbits so distant from mine that I could only guess whether Vanessa had a steady boyfriend—or if she fluttered through backyard parties and homecoming dances, humoring various admirers, her heart as famished as mine. What little I learned of her private life during those years made her appear all the more alluring—and less approachable. She was suspended two weeks in tenth grade for clawing the face of a cheerleader who'd threatened her younger sister. That same semester, she earned an unprecedented perfect score on Mr. Garson's trigonometry midterm, while I barely scraped a B-. In the spring, she made the county newspaper when she was sent home for wearing a T-shirt that proclaimed: *"Sex: The Anti-Drug."* To the interviewer at the *Star-Sentinel*, she described herself as "an ordinary, shy girl" who "had the most amazing parents in the world" and "just wanted to be a pediatrician." Most of my classmates planned to become fashion models and film directors and billionaires.

So I worshipped Vanessa Vidalgo from a remote distance. Then one autumn morning at the start of eleventh grade, I trudged downstairs for breakfast—which for me meant a cold Pop-Tart with root beer—and I found Vanessa seated on the leather armchair in our living room. My father was standing beside her, leaning across her enchanting body as though listening to a secret. I instantly realized what had happened: She'd discovered my role in Marty's stalking, and she'd come to report us. So I was already concocting excuses for our daily presence on Saratoga Street, when my father stepped away from the armchair, and I spotted the cylinder of dark blood pinched between his thumb and index finger. Vanessa smiled at me easily, without a hint of self-consciousness, just as she'd done four years earlier at the summer cocktail party. She had her left sleeve rolled up, exposing the perfectly smooth white flesh along her inner forearm. Even glimpsing her naked elbow filled me with guilt.

"Oh, there you are, Zachary," said my father. "So we won't have to dispatch the cavalry, after all." He tucked the tube of blood into the breast pocket of his shirt, alongside two other identical vials. "I was just telling Vanessa here about how you used to hide from girls as a toddler."

My father acted as though Vanessa's presence was nothing unusual, as though every morning we played host to a different teenage heartthrob. It still astounds me how a nationally-renowned oncologist with such a remarkably generous spirit always chanced upon precisely the wrong thing to say.

"Thanks, Dad," I said. "I owe you one."

I rolled my eyes for Vanessa's benefit. She beamed.

"Your father is hilarious, Zach," she said.

The moment called for a witty response; my tongue felt anchored to concrete.

"Vanessa's going to be having some weekly blood work done for at least the next few months," said my father. "It's easier for Rita Vidalgo to drop her off here, rather than going all the way to the clinic, so I said you'd give her a lift to school. You don't mind driving a pretty girl around, do you?"

"Whatever you want," I answered, struggling to sound nonchalant, "but we should really get going."

Vanessa rolled down her sleeve and hopped out of the armchair—the same sagging, stiff-backed chair where I had endured countless throat cultures and vaccinations. My father gave her shoulder a reassuring, paternal squeeze, and she followed me through the cluttered kitchen and down the patio steps to the driveway. I rushed to clear the crushed Pepsi cans and discarded popsicle sticks from the passenger seat, then retrieved a cotton beach blanket from the trunk and draped it across the sticky upholstery. When we pulled into traffic, I became acutely aware that the car—a hand-me-down Cadillac sedan from my mother—stank pungently of cigarette smoke and sweat. It was practically a locker room on wheels. I kept my gaze glued to the cracked windshield, but the corner of my eye snagged a peek at Vanessa's bare thigh.

"It's so sweet of your father to help me out like this," said Vanessa. "I can't tell you how grateful I am."

"Dad's a good guy," I said. "Both my parents are good people."

"He's very proud of you," said Vanessa. "You should have heard how he bragged about your archery trophies."

Our conversation felt very adult-like, serious—so different from the good-natured jabs I exchanged with my male friends.

"And I really appreciate you driving me," she added. "My mom has to be in Creve Coeur by eight at the latest—she's a teller at the Citizens Bank—so there's really no way she could get me to the clinic and back to school."

I already knew where Vanessa's mom worked. What I'd never really thought about was what this meant—that the *real* reason Vanessa needed a ride to school was that she didn't have a car of her own. I lacked the courage to ask Vanessa the cause for her blood tests, so I struggled for something else to say. All I could think of was how much I regretted not cleaning out the Cadillac. If nothing else, I'd have removed the figurines of celebrated archers that I'd glued to the dashboard—the miniature, un-matching statuettes of Apollo, Cupid, Robin Hood and William Tell, which had once defined the vehicle as mine, and suddenly seemed juvenile.

We crossed the avenues named after celebrated admirals—Farragut, Decatur, John Paul Jones—though none had any connection to Amity Cove. Pumpkins crowded the pine-board tables in front of Bonner's Outdoor Market. A blue-and-white banner hung from the roof of the reformed synagogue, greeting the Jewish New Year. I followed a slight detour along the waterfront, trying to avoid Saratoga Street, so instead we passed the chained gates of the amusement park, already deserted for the season, and the towering wooden loops of its landmark Thunder Coaster. We were only a few traffic lights from the school when Vanessa asked, "Can we do something crazy?"

She leaned toward me, and my entire body trembled. "I guess," I said.

"You promise you won't make fun of me?"

"I swear I won't," I agreed—too earnestly. "Honest."

"Can we drive past the firehouse?" asked Vanessa. She turned toward the passenger window, unwilling to meet my gaze, but she couldn't hide the swell of color in her neck. "I always walk by in the morning, just to check…"

I longed to press the back of my hand against her cheek, to feel its warmth. Instead, I veered the Cadillac onto Cowpens Street and looped behind the library into the center of town.

Amity Cove's brick-and-mortar, eighteenth-century fire station—originally built as an armory—occupied one face of the public common, so close to the high school that we could hear the alarms during gym class. The ornate clock tower, with latticework by Paul Revere, drew Revolutionary War buffs from across New England. That morning, both engines stood silent in their bays, glistening like children's toys under the morning light. Nearby, the flag fluttered at half-mast over the memorial for the village's World War dead, honoring a state trooper killed on duty.

"I know you must think I'm totally nuts," said Vanessa, "but I like to make sure my dad's okay before school starts—that the trucks are still there. Some days, I walk over at lunch to double-check. You won't tell people, will you?"

I might have offered to drive her at lunchtime, but I wasn't thinking clearly.

"I won't say a word," I promised.

"Thanks, Zach," she said. "I owe you."

These were the exact same words she repeated, verbatim, her dark lashes fluttering innocently, when I dropped her off in the unpaved parking lot opposite the varsity baseball field. I urged Vanessa to go on ahead, claiming I had to check the oil level under the hood. In reality, after years of a yearning so strong that I avoided this girl in the hallways, I didn't have the nerve to accompany her into the building.

Later that afternoon, when we passed on the stairs, Vanessa flashed a smile at me—a gentle, appreciative smile, offered fleetingly through her ocean of laughing and shouting friends. She didn't say anything, but she did have to. I already knew about her daily visits to the firehouse, a secret I wouldn't even disclose to Marty Kleetz, and this intimate gem buoyed me giddily through the remainder of the week.

· · · · ·

I counted down the days—the hours—until the next Monday morning. That Sunday night, my father knocked on my bedroom door and entered without waiting for an invitation. He'd been on call at the hospital all weekend, but at home he'd changed from his cardigan vest and bowtie into dungarees and a sweatshirt—a transformation that left him looking diminished. Luckily, when he'd intruded, all I'd been doing was lying in bed and daydreaming about my upcoming drive to school.

My father removed several target arrows and a damaged kite from the desk chair, and seated himself opposite the bed. He thumbed through books stacked beside the clock-radio, science fiction novels I'd borrowed from Marty. I kept my class reading in my knapsack and my private stash of "adult" fiction under the mattress.

"It's very helpful of you to take Vanessa to school," he said.

"Not a big deal," I answered.

I was thrilled to drive her, of course—but mortified to *talk* about it.

"She's a nice girl. They've had a hard time of it, you know. Al had that brother killed fighting those fires in Yellowstone—and now for this to happen," said my father. He sounded genuinely troubled, a departure from his usually unflappable placidity. This was the first I'd ever heard of Vanessa's uncle, or his death. "You haven't told anybody about the blood work, Zachary, have you?"

"Not a soul," I said. What I had done was to spend six hours in the reference section of the library, looking up maladies that required frequent blood sampling, but I didn't feel the need to mention this. "Why? What's wrong with her?"

"I'm glad you haven't told anyone. I'm not sure how the Vidalgos are handling all this, but I wouldn't want to make things worse for them." My father stood up decisively and patted my knee. "Your Grandpa Irving used to say that discretion is the hallmark of wisdom, but it's more the hallmark of decency. I suppose we might make a doctor of you yet."

"I want to be a professional archer."

My father didn't answer me directly. He strode to the door, jiggling his keys in his pants pocket. "Lovely girl. Very pretty," he said. "She'd make a fine girlfriend for you, if she weren't so sick."

. . . . .

The next morning, Vanessa showed up with her father. Al Vidalgo stood well over six feet tall, but he looked slender as a fire pole, and a large portion of his height was in his neck. His steel-rimmed glasses and Errol Flynn mustache were more suggestive of a mathematics professor than a firefighter. I watched through the Venetian blinds in the living room, where I'd been waiting for over an hour, while the pair climbed out of the fire chief's official vehicle and advanced up the flagstone walk. I hadn't counted on Vanessa's father giving her a lift. That made me thoroughly expendable, and all of my earlier joy evaporated into darkness.

I let my father answer the front door. Vanessa walked straight to the armchair and coiled up her sleeve. Over the weekend, she'd had her hair braided into cornrows and threaded through fluorescent beads.

Al Vidalgo shook hands with both my father and me.

"I hear you're an archer," he said.

"State champion," my father interjected. "Two years running."

I shot him a look as deadly as a poison-tipped arrow, but he was already focused on his patient, swabbing her skin with alcohol. My father leaned his shoulders forward, blocking my view of Vanessa's extended arm. A moment later, she winced. The fire chief stared off in the opposite direction, cupping a fist, waiting anxiously for the procedure to end.

"You should come out duck hunting with us one of these week-ends," Vidalgo said to me. "See how you handle a 9-bolt rifle. . . . We could use a good shot."

Guns were as much a part of my life as alchemy or space travel. I promised to visit his family's hunting blind as soon as school let out, though I knew I never would.

"Zach doesn't want to go shooting with a bunch of old men," said Vanessa. "I'm sure he has better things to do."

"So I'm an old man, am I?"

"But I love you anyway, Dad," said Vanessa. "Ready to roll?"

"You get a ride with Zachary, honey," Vidalgo answered. "I want to stick around for a few minutes and have a chat with Dr. Landon."

So Vanessa kissed her father on the cheek—which made me admire her all the more, although this was something that I would never have done myself—and I led her down to the driveway. I can't fully convey how grateful I was to be out of the house, not only on account of my father's knack for embarrassing me, but because I feared my mother, who slept late on the mornings she didn't play duplicate bridge or paddle tennis, might appear sporting only her all-too-sheer nightgown. The afternoon was breezy, but cloudless, and dried leaves swirled on the neighbor's lawns. Inside the Cadillac, the air now smelled fragrantly of lemon and spruce—with only a hint of stale tobacco.

"Your little statues are gone," said Vanessa.

I shrugged. "I did some cleaning."

"That's too bad. I liked them."

Vanessa trailed her delicate fingers along the dashboard, where scars remained from the rubber cement. "I like *everything* about your family, Zach," she said. "It must be awesome to have a father who's a doctor."

"Yeah," I snapped. "Unless you want to be a professional archer."

"I didn't know people did that."

"You sound like my dad." My words came out harsher than I'd intended, so I added, "There are national tournaments every weekend. Same as golf and tennis."

"Then you should win one," said Vanessa. "But don't be too hard on your father. Anyone can tell he wants the best for you."

This was my first exposure to Vanessa's willful blindness—her infuriating ability to gloss over misfortune. This was also the first time I had to confront the disturbing realization that she was anything less than perfect. Of course, her rosy glasses wouldn't have stopped me from eloping with her, but I was suddenly aware that this flesh-and-blood human being was more complex than the girl of my fantasies. We drove in silence along Pershing Street as I came to terms with this newfound reality. When we passed the gates of the amusement park and I accelerated into the traffic rotary, I nearly mowed down a jogger, but Vanessa didn't even notice. Nor did she ask me to drive past the fire station, because her father was still in my house, but I wish she had.

"Papa is worried about me," she said. "That's why he dropped me off today. He wanted to ask your dad more questions when my mother wasn't around."

I pulled into the high school parking lot. Dew glistened off the ball fields.

"Would it be prying if I asked what's wrong with you?"

She pursed her lips, puzzled. Perspiration built in the grooves of my palms.

"Jesus, Zach. I have leukemia," she answered. "I thought you knew that."

Vanessa pronounced the word leukemia with such upbeat cheer that it didn't sound like a disease. More like a distinctive talent. My initial reaction wasn't sadness, or sympathy, but self-pity: I felt like

the only human being on the entire goddam planet who hadn't
already known how sick she was.

. . . . .

I spent every free moment during the next three days in the
high school library, researching lymphocytes and oncogenesis, as
though a better understanding of Vanessa's illness might draw us
closer together. That's where she found me, nose buried in Nya-
hay's *Diseases of the Blood and Lymph*, early Thursday afternoon.
Vanessa wore baggy shorts and a men's tank top that revealed a
deep yellow bruise across her shoulder. Her hair was matted to her
forehead with sweat. She'd clearly come straight from gym class,
although the medical encyclopedia warned patients in her condition against excessive exertion.

"I'm *so* glad I found you," she said. "I need the biggest favor in
the world."

Her voice throbbed with desperation. Her breasts rose and fell
rapidly with her breath. I was ready to donate platelets, bone marrow. At that moment, she could have had all the blood in my veins
for the asking.

I snapped shut my book and held it against my chest, concealing the title.

"I was in gym and the fire horn started sounding—and I just
had to find out what was happening," explained Vanessa. "Can you
please drive me? Quick?"

The school expected me to take a physics exam in twenty minutes. Instead, I raced at full speed to the parking lot, pausing only
to let Vanessa catch up. The Cadillac squealed miserably into
reverse, churning up dust and gravel. When we arrived at the firehouse, of course, one of the engines was long gone. I asked Vanessa if she wanted me to go inside the station and inquire where

the alarm had come from, but she shook her head. She was crying. "It's okay," she said between sobs. "Papa only goes out with *both* engines." Her entire body shook violently, pulsing to its own seismic rhythm.

"I'm sorry," Vanessa bawled. "I'm so sorry."

It was haunting to see her so vulnerable, so helpless. This was several years before my own father's death—before I would discover the volatility of success and the sanding effect of fear upon power.

I waited for Vanessa's tears to dry out. Eventually, the missing engine lumbered up Trafalgar Street, most likely returning from a false alarm or a drill, and Chief Vidalgo emerged through a side door to greet his men. He carried a clipboard under one arm and a Styrofoam coffee cup in the other hand. Vanessa ducked down instantly and ordered me to drive. *Anywhere!* So I circled around the block toward the high school, thinking once again of my physics exam. Vanessa wiped her mascara off her cheeks with a tissue.

"Can you ever forgive me for panicking like that?" she asked.

"It's not a big deal." I swallow and clenched my fists. "Say, do you think you might want to go with me to Amityland sometime?" The amusement park was the least threatening date I could think of—as it wouldn't be open again for months. "I haven't been on the Thunder Coaster since I was nine," I added. "I thought it might be fun."

I hated myself as soon as I'd asked the question. I focused my eyes on the gearshift, fighting back nausea. All was silent except for the purr of the battered engine and the angry drone of the interior fan.

"Honestly, I'm afraid of Amityland," answered Vanessa. "Papa says the entire place is a giant fire trap." She shuddered. "I keep picturing him climbing onto those old wooden rides with flames and smoke all around him. . . . Maybe I'm going crazy."

I didn't push the matter further. She hadn't said yes. But, as far as I was concerned, she hadn't actually said no.

. . . . .

The following months were a rollercoaster of bliss and heartbreak. I continued to drive Vanessa to school on Monday mornings—and passed the remainder of my week scouring her every phrase for concealed meaning. No scholastic monk, poring over an ancient parchment, has labored any harder. Vanessa also enlisted my help, with increasing frequency, in tagging after the Amity Cove fire department. Al Vidalgo's daughter had mastered the complex language of the two-toned diaphone that moaned out the location of each suspected blaze, so we were consistently the third vehicle at alarm scenes—and one rainy afternoon, when coarse smoke billowed through the kitchen of Langer's deli, I actually pulled into the shopping center a good half-minute ahead of Vidalgo's men. But except for these excursions, I didn't see Vanessa outside of school. She spoke to me freely about her family life—Saturday picnics at her grandaunt's beach cottage, escorting her twin nieces to Mass on Sunday mornings—but she never mentioned the drinking parties she frequented on weekend nights, or the muscular, tattooed boys from neighboring towns who, in my worst nightmares, accompanied her to strip-poker games and narcotic-fueled orgies on the backs of the Harley-Davidson motorcycles. Over time, my invitation to the amusement park faded into memory.

By Thanksgiving, Vanessa's hair was gone. She took to wearing these tomboyish Pawtucket Red Sox caps that actually added to her sex appeal. In her bald state, her features appeared all the more flawless, like studies for a Renaissance sculpture. Only on the occasions when she wrapped a floral-print scarf around her scalp—usually mornings after she'd missed several days of school—did she appear sickly, as though training for a religious order that viewed beauty as shameful. In early December, she flew out to Minnesota to consult a specialist. Two weeks later, while my father and I were shoveling snow from the driveway, he informed me that I wouldn't be asked to drive Vanessa to school any longer. She was going to Episcopal Hospital in New York City for experimental therapy. Rhode Island's best physicians had nothing left to offer her.

The snow storm had started after midnight that Saturday, and by Sunday morning, the wet heavy drifts had buried the tops of the fire hydrants. I'd been looking forward all weekend to my twenty minutes alone with Vanessa—the interlude during which I refueled my psyche for the school week to come—so my father's calm, offhand tone shot straight to my blood. I jabbed my shovel into a snow bank. "She's going to die, isn't she?" I demanded. "Vanessa's going to die and none of you doctors give a damn."

My father looked up, surprised by my outburst. He rested his weight on the handle of his shovel, and let the low-hanging sky and the silence absorb my accusation. Thick moist flakes collected on his mustache and eyebrows. The tumor that would kill him was already creeping along the lining of his colon.

"Well, Dr. Landon?" I shouted. "Is she going to die or isn't she?"

"You know I can't answer that, Zachary." He plowed his shovel through the snow and heaved a sheet of ice into the hedges, then braced his body against the bumper of my mother's Volvo while recapturing his breath. "Physicians aren't miracle workers. We do our best." Here my father stopped, as though deciding whether to say more. "Medicine is the noblest calling in the world—I truly believe that—but in terms of knowledge, we're still in our infancy."

I couldn't see what was so noble about wandering around a hospital all day long, looking into strangers' throats and sticking fingers up their asses. It was lots of glorified patchwork and plumbing, as far as I was concerned. But I didn't dare express this, not to the man who had MD plates on his bicycle.

So Vanessa went off to Manhattan and I struggled on in Amity Cove. After my flare-up with my father, for which I apologized profusely the next morning, Vanessa became a taboo subject in our household. I didn't dare ask how her treatments were progressing, both ashamed of my earlier conduct and afraid to expose my feelings further. When my mother retired from the Board of Selectman in January, to devote herself fulltime to her bridge club, that severed another link between ourselves and the Vidalgos. At school, Marty never mentioned Vanessa. He'd acquired his own driver's license and had started hanging out with a ninth-grade tuba player named Angie. The two of them were already planning their marriage by the third date, which left the pair little time for scouting missions along Saratoga Street. None of Vanessa's popular friends knew about our excursions to alarm scenes, or anything about our relationship, so I couldn't reasonably expect them to update me on her care. For nearly a month, I survived on a diet of solo swings past the fire station and clippings about Al Vidalgo in the "Emergency Response" blotters of the *Cove Clarion* and the *Star-Sentinel*.

I managed to hold my emotions in check until Martin Luther King Day. That morning, after my father had left for his clinic, I fueled up the Cadillac and drove three hours straight to New York City. I'd only been there once before—on a sixth-grade field trip to the Statue of Liberty and Ellis Island—so it was nearly two o'clock by the time I gained my bearings and located the hospital. I parked at a metered space, opposite a laundromat. Customers, mostly beleaguered, middle-aged women, entered hauling sacks of clothing. Some wheeled their washables in wire carts; others brought along multitudes of well-fed toddlers. I waited in the car, the heat running, watching visitors pass through the revolving doors of the nearby Pediatric Pavilion.

These were the rightful guests of the sick and wounded. Relatives and close friends with a purpose—a justification—for visiting the hospital. In contrast, I was some dopey kid with an unrequited crush who'd driven across three states to visit a girl he hardly knew—a girl who, in all likelihood, had no desire to see him. So I couldn't muster the guts to go inside. When dusk settled over the neighborhood, I flipped on my headlights and drove back to Amity Cove.

. . . . .

College coaches came recruiting that February, accompanying me to the archery range to assess my technique. They never once asked me about my physics grades or the trajectory of objects shot from cannons. Marty and I spent winter break at his cousin's lodge in Maine, and we discovered ice fishing. On the same trip, I developed an interest in the older sister of Angie the Tuba Player, a sophomore at Vassar, who hardly knew that I existed. Slowly, as though she actually had died, Vanessa occupied my thoughts with increasingly less frequency. When my own popularity increased, and my career path loomed clearer, I forgot the pit of pain that I'd once suffered every time I imagined Vanessa kissing another guy behind the library. She was like a figment from early childhood, the vestige of an ethereal mirage. Only the empty desks in the classes we'd once shared confirmed that she'd ever existed at all. And then one damp, bone-chilling Monday morning in early March, as I was carving the name of Angie's sister into my mathematics notebook, Vanessa appeared in our first period calculus class.

. . . . .

The girl who returned to us that spring was, physically speaking, a husk of the untouchable creature who'd kept my friends from sleeping. Her once-exquisite skin had tightened in some places and loosened in others, forming irregular pockets of flesh beneath her eyes and under her chin. She wore long sleeves and a turtleneck sweater, but these were not enough to conceal the welts along her jaw and the backs of her hands. Most striking, she'd lost at least half of her body weight. Gone were the luscious curves that had rendered us tongue-tied. If I had met this girl for the first time that morning, I might have pitied her for her looks. Having worshipped her for half a decade, she remained to me, even in her ailing state, breathtakingly alluring. I took one look at Vanessa, waving to a friend across the classroom, and I couldn't comprehend how I'd ever been willing to settle for Angie the Tuba Player's sister.

When Vanessa and I crossed paths on the stairway that after-noon, I didn't let her escape with only a smile. Maybe it was her physical condition that steeled my courage—a belief that, shorn of her conventional beauty, she might be willing to lower her romantic expectations. Or maybe it was that, with the Division I archery scholarships pouring in, I'd somehow cultivated a confi-dence of my own. All I know for certain is that when her girlfriends glided past and Vanessa served me her diaphanous smile, I reversed course and followed her up the steps.

"Welcome back," I said. "I missed our drives."

"Thanks," she answered, her voice hoarse and faint. "I'm glad I'm here."

"I thought you might want to hang out and catch up. Maybe go for a drive around town," I said—staring at a fixed point over her shoulder. "I'm free all day on Sunday. If you wanted, I could pick you up around three."

I sensed that Vanessa's girlfriends were staring at me. I was blocking traffic on the staircase and making a public ass of myself.

"A drive around town?" Vanessa echoed. The surprise in her tone was unmistakable. "Sure, Zach, I could do that."

"I'll pick you up at three o'clock," I said. "Sunday."

Then I darted into the current of students before Vanessa could respond, and I avoided her for the remainder of the week, petrified that she might reconsider.

. . . . .

Sunday arrived: a clear, harsh gasp of winter. The wind howled through the shutters and slapped crabapple branches against the aluminum siding. I cruised up and down Saratoga Street, burning off fuel and time. When three o'clock arrived, Vanessa appeared on her porch and climbed down the stairs to meet me. She walked slowly, painfully so, bundled inside a shapeless beige coat. I crossed around to the passenger's door, like a chauffeur, and closed it behind her. This wasn't chivalry. I was sincerely afraid she didn't have the strength to do it on her own.

We had a snack at the Quahog Diner. This long, low-slung grease-joint had been the social hub of my junior high school years, where good-looking popular boys had taken good-looking popular girls, so I couldn't resist a triumphant return with Vanessa at my side. Many of the customers that afternoon were pre-teens recovering from recreation-league basketball games—and they stared at Vanessa. She didn't seem to care. I suppose she still thought like a beautiful girl. For the next two hours, we talked about my archery scholarships, and what bullshit she'd missed in physics class, and how Mr. Garson, the trigonometry teacher, had been fired for groping one of the disabled students he'd been tutoring. I was afraid to say anything about Vanessa's illness, and she didn't bring it up. The closest we came to discussing her condition was when she ordered a chef's salad and a glass of cranberry juice, but then apologized for leaving both untouched. "That's the thing with diners," she said, laughing. "It all looks delicious when you see it on the menu." When the plates were cleared, I asked Vanessa if she was enjoying herself. "Of course," she insisted. "It's really great to see you." So I paid our check and then followed the rutted dirt road behind the public library across the one-lane iron bridge that led into the county woods. Soon, Vanessa and I were sitting together in a parked car at a shadowy corner of the nature preserve.

We were in a hickory thicket, partially shielded from the wind. In a nearby clearing, a raccoon scavenged at an overturned garbage bin. Finches and chickadees trilled in the undergrowth.

"I have a confession to make," I said. "I tried to visit you in the hospital."

"Did you really?"

"I drove all the way down to New York," I said "But I was afraid you wouldn't want to see me."

"That was silly. Why on earth wouldn't I want to see you?" asked Vanessa. "I probably wasn't there, though. I was mostly getting outpatient therapy."

"You weren't there?"

Vanessa shook her head. "I spent nearly all of my time in my grandmother's apartment, sleeping and watching television. And *worrying*. I called home at least ten times a day to make sure my father was safe."

The long sunlight glistened off Vanessa's cheek. I ached to kiss her.

"Thank you, by the way," she said. "You're a very loyal friend, Zach. I think it's important to say thank you while you can. So, thank you."

Nothing she did could have been kinder—or less romantic. I examined her face, so damaged, so perfect, my hope deflating with every passing breath. I considered kissing her by surprise, just pushing my lips against hers and seeing what happened. Maybe I would generate my own miracle. What else could I do? But while I was dreaming up these fantasy scenarios, which I'd never actually have had the audacity to carry out, Vanessa's body went rigid. I feared she might be in pain.

"Do you hear that?" she asked.

I heard it. A distant foghorn. After months of chasing fires, I knew exactly where it led. Vanessa didn't have to order me to drive. I responded instinctively, like a firefighter roused by an alarm. On our madcap dash across town, while I darted through stop signs and traffic lights, she pleaded and bargained with God.

We found the amusement park an inferno. The Thunder Coaster rose like a flaming dragon through the blinding white smoke. Sparks rained from the Ferris wheel over the historic boardwalk and died on the adjacent water. Families with young children had gathered around the park's gates, watching the complex burn. Both of Amity Cove's engines were parked in the traffic circle—along with dozens of trucks from all of the neighboring towns. Firemen shouted at each other, and at the onlookers, trying to make themselves heard above the crackle and roar of the blaze. Several labored to attach a hose to a hydrant. Others simply stood beneath the conflagration, necks craned, watching in awe. There were also ambulances—and at least several bodies laid out on stretchers. I did not see Al Vidalgo among the rescue workers.

Vanessa grabbed the elbow of a young fireman, one of a pair charged with keeping civilians from crowding too close to the flames.

"Where's my Papa?" she screamed. "Oh my God. Where's my Papa?"

"You can't go in there," ordered the sentry. "Please, stay back."

This was a sound warning. I could already feel the deadly heat against my eyes. But Vanessa attempted to walk past the fireman.

When he blocked her path, she put up a concerted fight. Her base-ball cap fell to the ground, exposing her bare skin.

"Over there," I shouted. She didn't hear me at first. "Look!"

Al Vidalgo was running across the concrete plaza, an off-balance silhouette emerging from the smoke and flames, but it appeared as though he were advancing in slow motion—as though he were limping through water. The fire chief had a human body slung over his shoulder. One of the teenager trespassers, we'd later learn, who'd accidentally started the blaze. Ash blackened Vidalgo's face, and somehow he'd lost one of his protective boots, but he was incontrovertibly alive.

When Vanessa saw that her father was safe, she stopped strug-gling, and the young fireman released her arms. On the other side of the mesh gates, smoldering cedar beams—many of them more than a century old—crashed through the blinding haze. Overhead, fierce sparks danced across the night sky. The towering firestorm cast a pink-orange glow onto Vanessa's naked scalp and, for a few brief moments, she was transformed, once again, into the most beautiful human being I have ever seen.

I placed my hand gently on her frail shoulder—the only time we would ever touch—an act of compassion, not romance. Vanessa placed her opposite hand on top of mine, a gesture of warmth and gratitude. We stood there together, waiting, joined for a transitory moment. I already foresaw what the future held for each of us. I understood that I would become a physician like my father, heal-ing and curing as best as I could, and offering comfort when rescue was no longer possible.

Helen of Sparta

· ·

Laney Beck came to stay with us the autumn that my older brother, Darren, turned sixteen and insufferable. It had been a torrid summer—the second hottest on record along Florida's Gulf Coast—so dry that the freshwater pond behind our motel withered into caked, cracking earth. Carcasses of alligators and armadillos lined the parched drainage ditches along the roadbeds. Sea grapes shriveled in black clusters. But Darren's fixation that August was the shape of his ears, how one curved up gently like the sheath of a fig shell, while the other rose to an elfin point. He studied his reflection at every opportunity: in shop windows, swimming pools, the Plexiglas faces of vending machines. He tried to "cure" the deviant ear with a convex brace fashioned from pipe cleaners. My brother's other obsession was driving, and he was all-too-willing to chauffeur me to junior tango practice and oboe lessons as a pretext to borrow Mama's Taurus. Or, if it meant extra time behind the wheel, to pick up Laney Beck from the airport in Fort Myers.

So that's how it happened. Darren volunteered and I went with him. Not by choice, of course. But the day after Columbus Day was Superintendent's Conference Day in the Lee County schools, which meant that big brothers all over Cormorant Island were saddled babysitting their twelve-year-old sisters. Mama had wanted to drive out to the airport herself—Laney Beck was her oldest friend, after all, her only *real* friend—yet with Papa still up in St. Petersburg, tending to Aunt Pricilla, she didn't trust my brother to man the motel office solo. Especially not on a Tuesday, when the linens went out.

Darren drove for speed, not accuracy. At the traffic lights, he flipped down the ceiling mirror and scoured his face for blemishes. At the longer lights on Nautilus Boulevard, he filed his fingernails. I've always felt a twinge of terror crossing bridges, and cruising over the causeway to the mainland at twice the posted limit, I dug my fingernails deep into the vinyl upholstery. But I knew not to beg Darren to be careful. That was a guaranteed way to make him hit the gas.

As we approached the airport, following the complex sequence of lane shifts that wound past the permanently-shuttered Air Force Museum and the dusty civil aviation field, heavier traffic forced my brother to slow down. "I've got a million-dollar proposition for you, Wunderkind," he said.

"Give me the million dollars first," I answered.

"Cute, real cute. Seriously, parking is going to be hell. How would you feel about running inside and finding her?"

"Didn't Mom give you money for the lot?"

Darren made a nasty face at me. "C'mon, Wunderkind. We're past the turnoff for the garage. I'll have to drive all the way through the loop again."

He swerved around a stand of orange construction barrels, honked at a Hertz shuttle bus, and came to a screeching halt inches from the curb. We were in front of the arrivals terminal, a steel-and-concrete structure whose dramatic curves might have seemed futuristic in the sixties—but, by the Reagan era, had acquired the gloom of unrealized ambitions. Ailanthus shoots poked through the cracks in the asphalt. Darren and I hadn't yet reached an agreement. I folded my arms across my flat chest and stared out the passenger-side window.

A crowd had gathered around the terminal's automatic doors, between the smokers' benches and the curbside check-in. Music streamed from an overhead speaker: Billie Holiday crooning "Summertime." On the sidewalk below, a strawberry blonde in sandals was slow-dancing with a skycap. She appeared to be leading. Only when a second skycap grabbed the woman's waist, and attempted to pry her from the first, did I recognize the woman from the photographs: It was Laney Beck! And she wasn't exactly dancing. More like staggering. My mother's girlhood friend clung onto her "dance partner" like a woman afraid of toppling from a steep precipice.

The skycap's cap fell off and rolled under a taxicab. The automatic doors swung open and shut, open and shut, in an apocalyptic rhythm. "Jesus Christ. Somebody get security," shouted the second skycap.

And then my brother was out of the Taurus and pressing his way through the crowd. "It's okay," he called out. "She's with us." He said something to Laney Beck and she released her hold on the skycap. The bag agent turned out to be a lanky black man in his sixties with a gray brush mustache. Darren took the parking money—it must have been twenty dollars—and stuffed it into the man's hand. The next thing I knew, I was in the backseat between Laney Beck's golf clubs and her hatbox, and the three of us were racing toward the airport exit at top speed.

. . . . .

"Such excitement!" exclaimed Laney Beck. "And I haven't even been on the ground for half an hour."

Laney Beck spoke as though she were accustomed to this sort of excitement, as if, whenever she traveled, it was her habit to jump airport personnel. She reached for her sunglasses, perched atop her frenzied hair, but one of the mirrored lenses had chipped. "I do believe that man broke my glasses," she said—more surprised than upset. "Luckily for me, I have a spare set somewhere. Take that as a word of wisdom from your Cousin Laney: Always carry a second pair of glasses. And dentures, too. Though I don't suppose any of us need to worry about that just yet." Laney Beck, who was *not* our biological cousin, rummaged through her oversized handbag, which jingled with coins, and drew out an identical pair of glasses. She placed them over her enormous eyes, and laughed—an innocent, girlish laugh. Then she lowered her voice, like a young child about to reveal a secret. "I have a horrible confession to make," she said. "I'm so terrified of flying, I drank those little bottles of scotch until they cut me off."

"Not a big deal," said Darren. "We'll have you home in twenty minutes."

"Twenty minutes?" Laney responded. "Oh, I can't let your mother see me like this. It's already bad enough that I'm imposing on such short notice."

It *had* been rather sudden. Laney Beck's second marriage had collapsed and she'd phoned Mama—out of the blue—to see if she could "borrow a room" at the Jolly Roger for a couple of weeks. Just to "sort through her thoughts." Before that, they'd spoken on the phone every few months, and they'd exchanged holiday gifts religiously, but they hadn't actually *seen* each other since many years earlier, when Laney starred as Ophelia at the Performing Arts Center in Tampa. Now, Mama's friend was old enough to play Hamlet's mother. But from what I understood, nobody in New York was asking her to play much of anything.

Darren kept driving. We pulled onto the state highway, where a brush fire had charred out several hundred acres of pine scrub. The wind had picked up—a cold front blowing in off the Gulf—and angry clouds cloaked the horizon.

"Everything looks so different," said Laney. "All these shopping plazas. When your mother and I were girls, this entire area was just swamp and avocado farms. Nobody in their right mind traveled south of Sarasota—unless it was to fool around on the beach. Or—did your mother ever tell you about the time this guy Chuck Grambly took us to a cock fight? A real live cock fight *with roosters.*"

"No, she didn't," said Darren.

"Well, he did. With friends of his from the tackle shop—straight out of *Deliverance.* . . . He had a crush on me, Chuck Grambly," said Laney, smiling. "Meanwhile, I can't get over how big you two have gotten. I hardly recognized you. How old were you last time I saw you, Amanda, dear? Four? Five? You probably don't even remember."

I wasn't sure how to answer. I was certain—*mathematically* certain—that I'd *never* before met Laney Beck.

"You look just like your mother, dear," she said. "Spitting image. I could pick Melanie Shunt's girl out of crowd with my eyes closed."

It took me a moment to register that Melanie Shunt was my mother. Melanie *Rothmeyer.* I don't think I'd ever heard anyone use her maiden name before. Or say that I looked like her, though we shared the same broad forehead.

"*Everything* has changed. That's what happens when you're past thirty," said Laney. "Do you two go to high school at Thomas Edison?"

"I go to Francis Scott Key," answered Darren. "I'm almost done. She goes to the middle school on Cormorant Island."

"Well, *I* went to Thomas Edison. Up in Sarasota. I studied dramatic writing with Mrs. Gonchette. I wonder if she's still teaching," said Laney Beck. "She'd be passed retirement age, of course—but lots of teachers stay on into their seventies."

"I'm thinking of becoming a doctor," said Darren. "Maybe a plastic surgeon."

"Wherever life takes you, darling," Laney Beck answered non-committally. "I have an idea. Let's go there. To Thomas Edison. It's not that far."

I could not have been more shocked if Laney Beck had proposed a road trip to California—or Continental Europe. In our family, this was the sort of outing planned weeks in advance.

"What do you say, Wunderkind?" asked Darren.

"You told Mama we'd come straight home," I said. "She'll want the car."

"I'm sure she'll understand, Amanda. We've always been share-and-share-alike, your mother and I," answered Laney Beck. She turned to my brother. "Please, Darren. For me. . . . It'll give me a chance to dry out. And I promise we'll have fun."

Darren didn't say another word. But he pulled off the state highway at the next exit, and followed the signs for I-75 North to Sarasota.

· · · · ·

Thomas Edison Consolidated High School was a low-slung, red brick building surrounded by a high mesh fence. Two wings—one cinderblock, the other stucco—marked successive expansions in the fifties and seventies. There was also a phalanx of white box trailers on a nearby field that housed either makeshift offices or overflow classrooms. The complex reminded me of an internment camp. But since we'd crossed the county line, school was in session. Two bare-chested guys were tossing around a fluorescent pink Fris-bee on the traffic island out front. More kids were sitting at nearby picnic tables, eating bag lunches. I felt suddenly important, being a visitor and not a student. I suspect Darren experienced something similar, because he drove straight past the elderly parking officer and pulled into the lot marked "STAFF ONLY." At his own school, Francis Scott Key, that got you suspended. But the last laugh was on us, because the remaining empty spaces were at the far end of the macadam—nearly a football field's length away. As we hiked back toward the school, a cold, lashing rain started falling. It peppered the adjacent manmade lake like an artillery barrage. When we finally entered the building's main entrance, our clothing was thoroughly soaked.

Two trophy cases lined the vestibule. A large black-and-gold banner, hanging directly in front of us, read: "Edison Panthers, State Champions, 1977." It didn't say what they had won. Group photographs of long-forgotten athletic teams formed a wainscoting along the corridor. Varsity Baseball, 1957. Women's Track and Field, 1958. One end of the short hall led to a staircase, the other into a modern office suite. A teenage couple leaned against a nearby stand of lockers, kissing. The guy was hot.

"It all looks so different," said Laney Beck. "It even *smells* different."

I took a deep sniff of air. It smelled faintly of cigarette smoke and chlorine.

"Where to?" asked Darren.

"It's a little bit overwhelming," answered Laney Beck. "This area used to be the Student Commons. I don't remember all these offices." To my amazement, she walked directly up to the kissing couple, and asked: "Do you know where Mrs. Gonchette's classroom is?" I could have died from shame.

The hot guy looked up. Surprised, maybe. But too suave to be embarrassed. "Does she teach chemistry?"

"Dramatic writing," said Laney Beck.

"Hmmm. Maybe in the annex," he answered. The girl shifted her weight from one slender leg to the other, and said nothing.

"Thank you, darling," said Laney Beck. She walked back to us, and the teenage couple disappeared up the stairs. "I remember now," she said decisively, pointing like a marshal on a battlefield. "It's that way."

Laney Beck started down a nearby passageway, and we followed. We'd hardly gotten twenty yards, when an authoritative voice called after us. It belonged to a hulking, red-faced security officer. He rested one hand atop the flashlight on his belt, as though, in an emergency, he could draw it as a gun.

"Can I help you, ma'am?" he asked.

"Oh, no," answered Laney. "We're just visiting." She paused for a moment, maybe deciding whether more explanation was called for. "I went to school here," she added. "I've come to see an old teacher."

Laney Beck and the guard faced off like gunslingers at high noon.

Suddenly, the guard sneezed. He removed a cloth handkerchief from his rear trouser pocket to shield his face, and he sneezed again. Maybe the man was allergic to Laney Beck's confidence. The two of them made me anxious.

"Okay," said the guard. "But all visitors have to check in at the main office."

"Oh, we've done that. All taken care of," lied Laney.

Then she smiled—the same benign, wholly disarming smile that had convinced Darren to drive her to Sarasota—and she strode off down the passageway.

"Ma'am, I need to see your passes," the guard called after her. Laney ignored him. She kept walking, more determined now. I looked at Darren for guidance, and he shrugged. So we scrambled to catch up with Laney, and let her lead us down another short staircase, and between two science laboratories, chock-full of bottled specimens, to a concourse of older classrooms.

It was so hard to believe that this zany, fearless woman who danced with skycaps and lied to security guards was Mama's best friend. I loved my mother dearly, but she was about as far from zany or fearless as they came. She'd studied accounting for two years at the State University, then married a business degree student twelve years her senior. They'd purchased a beachfront motel with Papa's savings from his work as a bank manager and the bulk of her own father's life insurance. Nothing glamorous about it. My parents had also considered a restaurant, and even a bed-and-breakfast, but Papa thought a motel less risky. So sometimes when Mama spoke of Laney Beck—her popularity at Pembroke, her Peace Corps stint in the Cameroon, her theatrical triumphs in Boston and then New York City—I couldn't help holding it against Mama that she hadn't had similar victories. That she'd never even *tried*. Or course, if Mama had gone off to New England, and married a professional ice skater, I would never have existed.

"That's her classroom," said Laney. "On the right."

The door to the classroom on the right stood wide open. Rows of students sat perpendicular to the entryway, listening to a lesson in Greek mythology. Beyond them, the driving rain pounded against the floor-to-ceiling windows. We approached the door and several of the students glanced in our direction. The teacher continued speaking in a high-pitched, nasal voice. She was sharing a story from her own youth—about how she'd sobbed the first time she read the myth of Demeter and Persephone. The woman was small, waifish, in her twenties. She was clearly not the celebrated Mrs. Gonchette.

A coffee mug on the cluttered desk was labeled Carol's Brew. One of the students asked a question about Hades; he addressed the teacher as Miss McBride.

"Maybe Mrs. Gonchette switched classrooms," I whispered.

Laney Beck waved her fingers at a long-haired boy who was watching us, and the kid looked away quickly. "Let's go listen in," Laney suggested. And without any further warning, our guide stepped into the classroom and took up a position along the rear wall. Darren and I followed, as though entranced. I stared at the carpet, afraid to make eye contact with the young teacher. Eventually, I let my gaze wander sideways: over the legs of the students in the back row and onto the stainless steel sink in the corner. I could not have been more nervous if we'd climbed through Miss McBride's bedroom window.

But the woman kept on teaching. She'd advanced through Persephone and Demeter to Daphne and Apollo. Her lesson drifted from history to legend to personal anecdote, including a digression about how she'd once had a crush on a laurel sapling. When I dared to look up, my face red and scorching, she was reading from Bulfinch's *The Age of Fable*. "Since you cannot be my wife," she declaimed, roleplaying Apollo, "You shall assuredly be my tree. I will wear you for my crown; I will decorate with you my harp and my quiver. And, as eternal youth is mine, you also shall be always green, and your leaf shall know no decay..." Every few passages, the tiny woman peeked up and offered us a puzzled glance. She appeared fresh to her job, and somewhat uncertain of herself.

I looked over at Darren. He was focused on the tanned skin of the girl in front of him, whose cutoff T-shirt was riding up her back.

"Louise Gonchette had a wondrous reading voice," Laney Beck said under her breath. "Like melted sugar to the ears."

Carol McBride closed her battered copy of Bulfinch and wrapped a rubber band around it. She took two steps toward us—and then, apparently, thought the better of it. Instead, she ventured into a new anecdote. "I'll tell you all a secret," she said to her class. "When I was your age, I used to fantasize that *I* was Helen of Troy. So tell me—those of you who have done the homework reading—*who was* Helen of Troy?"

A round-faced girl in a faded lavender sweater raised her hand. "The most beautiful woman in the world."

Several students snickered. Either at the round-faced girl or at the prospect of Carol McBride being attractive.

"That's correct," Miss McBride said didactically. "Helen of Troy *was* the most beautiful woman in the world. She had a face to launch a thousand ships."

A bearded guy up front made a remark that I couldn't hear. Laughter rippled back toward us. Carol McBride blushed—and I felt genuinely bad for her. I sensed that our presence was adding to the restlessness of her students.

"*Many* teenage girls dream about being Helen of Troy," she said, matter-of-factly. "It's a rather common fantasy."

"Don't you mean Helen of Sparta?" interjected Laney Beck.

The room went silent. Carol McBride looked like she'd seen Medusa.

Laney stepped forward as though the classroom were her own.

"Her name was Helen *of Sparta*. The wife of King Menelaus. It's bad enough that she was carried off to Troy *against her will*. Changing her name in the historical record compounds her victimization." Laney Beck laughed—not her playful laugh, but more bitterly. "All of you should think about the implications of name changing. Especially you girls. I've been married twice, but I've always held on to my name."

The students looked at Laney Beck. Then they looked at Carol McBride.

"Who are you?" asked Miss McBride. "This is my classroom."

"Sorry I interrupted," said Laney. "Please don't mind us." She turned toward me and added, loudly, "I guess your Cousin Laney's become too political for her own good."

"Are you supposed to be here?" asked Miss McBride.

Laney braced her arm against the back of a chair. "We're just visiting. I came to see Louise Gonchette, but I guess she's no longer teaching."

This last statement had an unexpected effect on Carol McBride. She bit her thin lip and tapped her left hand nervously against her boyish hip. "You should check at the main office about Louise Gonchette," she said.

I peered up at Laney Beck and I could tell from her expression that she'd heard something in Carol McBride's mousy voice that I wasn't yet trained to hear. But I understood Laney's face: Louise Gonchette was dead.

At that moment, three uniformed men appeared in the entryway. One was the hulking, red-faced guard. The other two were full-fledged Sarasota police officers. They had real guns and Billy clubs, not flashlights, hanging from their belts. The bearded slacker in the front row exclaimed: "Shit. It's the cops!"

"That's her," said the red-faced guard.

"Please hold your hands where I can see them and step out of the classroom, ma'am," said the taller cop. This was the pre-Columbine era, and Laney Beck truly looked as harmless as a dove, but I guess these guys weren't taking any chances.

"I think we're in trouble," said Laney Beck. She did not raise her hands or walk toward the classroom door. In fact, she giggled. "I'm sorry you had to come all the way down here, officers. We were just on our way out."

The second cop stepped into the classroom, guarding us from the side. Or preparing to shield Miss McBride from gunshots.

The first cop said, "I'm not going to repeat myself again, ma'am. Place your hands where I can see them and step out of the classroom."

Darren raised his hands. I did the same, leaning flat against the chalkboard to avoid a potential crossfire.

"This is all a misunderstanding," said Laney Beck. "It's not like I'm not some kind of criminal."

The second cop approached Laney. He held a pair of handcuffs. The fluorescent lights made his bald pate look purple.

"Jack Finn!"

The bald cop stopped abruptly. He made an instinctive move for his gun.

"Jack Finn. It's me, Laney Beck. From school."

That pierced the second cop like a bullet. He clutched the handcuffs, as though afraid he might drop them, and rested his other hand on his holster.

"I don't know how I caused all this fuss," continued Laney, sounding remarkably innocent. "I'm visiting from New York...and I just came to see if Mrs. Gonchette was still teaching...I suppose I must have gone the wrong way or something..."

"Jeez," said the cop. "You *are* Laney Beck."

"That's what they keep telling me."

Jack Finn's eyes raked Laney from head to toe, practically absorbing her, like Humphrey Bogart might do with an old flame in a detective movie. He waved off the taller cop. "It's fine, Pete. She's all right."

"You sure?" asked the red-faced guard.

Jack Finn ignored this. He took Laney by the arm and led steered gently from the classroom. "I'm married now," he said. "Four boys."

"That's wonderful," said Laney—but she looked disappointed. "Boys are easier."

"I don't know about that," said Jack Finn. "But I love them."

Laney Beck winked at him. "So good to run into you," she said.

"Yeah. Good to see you, Laney." He still held onto her arm. "Say, you're not thinking of coming back here, are you?"

"Of course, not," she said. "Don't be silly."

And that was that. We walked down the corridor and through the high quadruple doors of the school's main entrance, the red-faced guard following us to the edge of the drenched macadam lot.

· · · · ·

Laney Beck was only marginally more subdued on the drive home to Cormorant Island. She flipped the car radio to an Oldies Station, and we caught the tail end of an hour-long tribute to Captain & Tennille. The rain had let up, and the wind was ebbing, but the temperature had dropped twenty degrees in a couple of hours. My clothes were still damp. I clenched my teeth together to keep them from chattering.

"Jack Finn used to write me love letters," said Laney Beck. "They were full of misspellings, but they were adorably sweet. He even tried to write me poems . . ."

"Did you go out with him?" asked Darren.

"Jack Finn. Lord, no," said Laney. "He wasn't my type. And way too earnest. Besides, I had my hands full in high school. . . . But I'm glad things have worked out so well for Jack."

"Sometimes it takes a while to figure out if someone is your type," said Darren. I sensed he was thinking wishfully about some popular girl who'd rejected him—not Laney Beck and Jack Finn. "Don't you think?"

"Not me. I've always known in ten minutes," answered Laney. "But for a long time, I thought Jack and your mother might have gotten on. I bet you don't know that we all went on a double date once..."

So we crossed over the causeway and onto Cormorant Island with Laney Beck recalling a twenty-year-old expedition to a bowling alley in Clearwater. One of the few places around that had dancing *and* served kids under eighteen. She acted as though nothing remarkable had happened in Sarasota—as though her encounter with Jack Finn had been purely social. Darren drove more carefully now. Maybe the cops had scared him. But I did catch him steeling peeks at his reflection in the mirrors. We hit rush hour traffic heading out of Fort Myers. I cannot express how relieved I was to pull onto the caked shell driveway of the Jolly Roger.

We threaded our way between the tennis courts and the bougainvillea hedge. A large ring-billed gull hopped across the road in front of us.

"I do hope I look presentable. I'm nervous as a schoolgirl," said Laney. "I trust you darlings won't tell your mother about those little scotch bottles..."

"Your secret is safe," said Darren.

He circled through the dunes beyond the shellfish washing hut, and the motel came into view over the beach grass. The maid's carts were all gone. It was after six o'clock. Mama waved to us from the upper landing. The car had hardly come to a stop when Laney charged up the wooden steps. Mama raced down to greet her. They met on the first floor balcony and embraced.

Darren and I watched from below. The breeze was still fierce down by the shoreline and the breakers crashed against the jetty. Skimmers circled overhead; a woodpecker drilled methodically in a nearby electric post. Whatever Laney Beck was explaining to Mama was lost to the roar of air and surf.

I leaned my elbows on the trunk of the Taurus.

"You were really great at the airport," I said. "I mean: really adult-like."

"I'm working on it," answered Darren—but I could tell he was pleased. And I was rather pleased too. Complimenting him made *me* feel like an adult.

My brother circled the car and patted my shoulder affectionately. We stood side-by-side in silence. Then Darren, in an intimate voice, asked, "She's beautiful, isn't she?"

"Who's beautiful?"

"Who do you think, Wunderkind?" The bite returned suddenly to my brother's voice. "Laney Beck."

I thought he was joking at first—but he obviously wasn't.

"Pervert!" I snapped. "She's as old as Mama."

"Sure, but Mama isn't—"

He let the unfinished sentence hang in the damp air. But it was true. She wasn't. And for the first time in my life, I saw how something that small could explain everything, what had happened before and what would come after.

The Bigamist's Accomplice

· ·

Arlene's husband offers her a pair of clay elephants and tells her that he intends to marry another woman. The elephants are quite finely wrought, she thinks, one African, the other Asian, although she can never remember which is which. Their meticulously proportioned features and gracefully curved trunks are a vestige of Benny's years sculpting human noses and chins to perfection. In contrast, one of the other elderly men in the television lounge has fashioned his wife a dromedary—"It's sitting down," he explains—but, to Arlene, the offering looks more like a lumpy, upturned breast. She is fiercely proud of her husband, even as she feeds him a box of grape juice through a miniature straw. She ignores his marriage plans. After thirty-seven years together, she is confident that this too shall pass, that the proposal is another unmoored plank afloat in the ocean of her husband's psyche. But then Benny swats away the juice box and squeezes the back of Arlene's hand. She can feel her arm trembling along with his. "I've decided to marry Connie," he says again. "Please don't let me forget."

"But you're already married *to me*," Arlene answers patiently. "It's Arlene."

Benny blinks his eyes—as though struck by an unwelcome burst of light. He frowns in obvious disappointment. "Am I really?" he asks. He gazes off toward the snow-caked courtyard beyond the bay windows, perplexed, embarrassed. Her husband has cheated on her in the past, Arlene knows—with a charge nurse named Beulah, with the mother of an adolescent patient, with others—but he's done so discreetly. This is the first time she has seen him openly ashamed of his desires. He drums his fingers on the table-top and mutters, to nobody in particular, "I thought I was going to marry Connie."

Arlene scans the lounge. The walls are papered in institutional pastels, punctuated by innocuous prints of sunflowers and migratory ducks; a low winter sun blazes between the slats of the Venetian blinds. It is hard to imagine any room on earth with less personality. All around Arlene sit women who have outlived their husbands, a pathetic sisterhood of fragility and diminished hopes. She is not jealous of Connie, she assures herself. Merely curious. Maybe she also feels a twinge of guilt, because she still teaches during the week and drives out to the Valhalla Home only on weekends. But why is that unreasonable? She's not even sixty. Isn't she entitled to maintain an existence of her own? Besides, Benny holds just the vaguest notions of who she is and why she visits. During the first few months, he wept like her kindergarten students each time she hugged him goodbye. But now, steeped in the marrow of his dementia, everything with Benny is out of sight, out of mind. So does it really matter which of these desiccated, memory-shorn creatures is the darling of her husband's senile fantasies? Her marriage has survived Beulah the charge nurse, Arlene reminds herself; she has a thirty-seven year advantage and a hundred IQ points over Connie the halfwit.

Benny starts suddenly, regal and wary like a bull elk. "Where's Arlene?" he demands.

"*I'm Arlene,*" answers Arlene.

He shakes his head vigorously. "Not you. The *other* Arlene."

She can sense he is thinking of Connie, but has already lost the woman's name.

"I am *the other* Arlene," Arlene lies. "I'm right here."

Her husband responds with a burst of laugher. He laughs, and laughs, until he looks up, suddenly confused, no longer certain of what he has found so funny.

. . . . .

The next day is Purim—the Feast of Esther—and Arlene bakes *hamantaschen*. She does this every winter—much as she stuffs blintzes on *Shavuos* and fries *matzoh brei* on Passover—not because she is religious, or even spiritual, but because she cannot conceive of doing otherwise, any more than she can imagine not lighting *yartzeit* candles for her departed parents. It helps that Benny still takes pleasure in food, that he is grateful for a carryout pastrami sandwich from the Riverdale Deli, even as he forgets that he has kept Kosher for sixty-two years. But when Arlene delivers the triangular pastries, an assortment of prune, apricot and poppy seed, she finds her husband talking surgical technique to *the other Arlene*. Connie is an oval-faced woman with her long gray hair parted down the middle like Olivia de Havilland in *Gone with the Wind*. She's older than Benny, somewhere on the far side of seventy. The two of them are sitting side-by-side in the poorly-lit corridor opposite the elevators, their wheelchairs touching obscenely, the companion with a wool blanket sheltering her knees and a bland smile plastered across her lips. Benny is expounding upon competing methods for performing otoplasty. As Arlene approaches, she sees that they are holding hands.

Her pulse quickens and she feels, for a moment, as though she's falling from a bridge. She's too sensible to cause a scene—she has always played superego to Benny's unbridled id—but she drops her jaw in a fraught, voiceless scream.

"They look happy together, don't they?"

The onlooker is a tall, distinguished gentleman in the last strides of middle age. He sports a plaid cap and a cardigan sweater. His mustache is nearly white, his bushy eyebrows a darker shade of gray.

"They're *not* a couple," protests Arlene. "That's my husband."

"I'm Jim Drapkin," the man answers, extending a hand. "I'm Connie's husband."

Arlene appraises Drapkin, dumbfounded. She clings to the tin of pastries like a life buoy.

Drapkin waves to his wife. Connie smiles. "I'm so glad they found each other," he says.

The idea that someone has "found" her husband, like a lost sock or an unclaimed island, leaves Arlene without words. She waits for Drapkin to explain himself further—*to explain that she has misunderstood him!*—but he merely nods approvingly at the demented couple, his hands tucked into the pockets of his trousers. A lanky workman carries a paint-splattered ladder out of the elevator and sets about changing one of the ceiling bulbs above the nurses' workstation. In the television lounge, a female voice shouts, "Bingo! I've got bingo!" Seconds later, another female voice answers, "Goddam bullshit. That's what you've got."

Arlene takes a deep breath. "How long has this been going on?" she demands.

"Connie's been here three weeks. She was in a day program before this, and then she spent a month at Presbyterian Hospital with a broken hip." Drapkin's tone is placid and benevolent, but detached—as though he's discussing a character in a film. "The first morning I came to visit her out here, your husband was already telling Connie his surgery stories. He makes her laugh, especially the way he talks with his hands." Drapkin leans forward and adds, in a hushed tone, "But to tell you the God's honest truth: I'm not so sure how much she understands anymore."

"I can't believe this," says Arlene. She feels her composure slipping between her fingers like sand. "Your wife's trying to seduce my husband—and you don't care!"

Drapkin flashes her a sharp look. "That's not fair. I'm out here every day, rain or shine, seven days a week." He pauses, collecting himself. "I love my wife as much as life itself. More than life itself. But I'm also a realist. Fifteen years sitting on the family court bench does that to a man. So trust me when I tell you that the two of them are lucky to have one another. Facilities like these are lonely places. A close friend can make all the difference."

The difference between what and what? Arlene wants to know. *And since when do friends hold hands in public like teenage lovers?* But she is also taken by the sincerity in the retired judge's deep, resonant voice. This is a man who *sounds* fair.

"I try to be forward-looking," he adds. "To keep my eyes on the future."

She glances from Judge Drapkin to the pair seated opposite the elevators. Her husband's shirt is buttoned incorrectly and the folds of his neck are poorly shaved. Often he forgets to ask the nursing staff to change his diaper. Yet this is the same man who returned from his stint in the navy's medical corps with her name inked across his biceps, who has made love to her on countless nights in luxury hotel suites, and opera house restrooms, and the backseats of rental cars across six continents. She watches him talking to his new companion, and is almost touched as he tucks a strand of steely hair behind the woman's ear. Benny looks contented, serene. But Arlene has been though too much—fought too many battles—to share her prize.

"This has to stop," she announces. She walks briskly across the corridor, takes hold of Benny's wheelchair, and steers her stunned husband into the television lounge. Then she storms back into the busy hallway. She is prepared to lay into Jim Drapkin—to warn him to keep his dopey wife away from her husband. But she catches sight of the nursing director, Annie Serspinski, playing dominos with one of the residents—a blind woman who reads the tiles like Braille—and Arlene decides that the times call for more desperate measures. Annie is a big tub of a woman in her thirties. She's efficient, devoted. Her entire life is the Valhalla Home, and she has a knack for anticipating trouble, as she does now, struggling onto her tree-trunk legs and approaching Arlene. "How is Dr. Steinhoff today?"

Arlene points her index finger at Connie Drapkin.

"I don't want that woman in the same room with my husband."

Annie nods and demands no further explanation. She clearly knows already. *Everybody* knows already, except Arlene, because she's been occupied teaching shapes to five year olds.

"I'll see what I can do," says the nursing director. "Are you sure about this?"

Arlene glares at Jim Drapkin. "I'm one hundred percent certain."

. . . . .

When she returns home to the Bronx that evening, Arlene tries to block the entire episode from her thoughts. She passes the next three nights preparing floor-to-ceiling calendars for her classroom walls, each date printed on its own construction paper cutout: scarves for March, umbrellas for April, daffodils for May. She usually fashions these displays one month in advance, maybe two, but now she works her way though June's flags and then the multicolored maple leaves for the following September. What else is there to do? She and Benny used to socialize as a couple: dinners out, contract bridge, doubles tennis in summer at the public courts. Beyond a certain age, the world isn't designed for solo travelers. Yet in the two years since Benny's diagnosis—multi-infarct dementia, not Alzheimer's, a distinction that matters only to pathologists—she has suddenly become one of those aging, ethnic widows who wander New York City's outer boroughs as their neighborhoods change over or die. She has pitied these forlorn creatures through the years, the elderly Irishwomen of Woodlawn, and the perpetually-mourning Italian grandmothers of Belmont, and those babushka-shrouded Polish ladies one passes outside funeral parlors in Greenpoint. Yet here she is living in Riverdale, alone, childless, an increasingly lax Jew now that Benny is away, surrounded by Orthodox starter couples, young mothers pushing an eternal phalanx of strollers. It doesn't help any that she is trapped in this peculiar limbo between marriage and widowhood—that well-meaning people have the gall to ask her whether she is "dating" again, as though her husband's life has been reduced to a sideshow. Arlene is tracing October's jack-o-lanterns, wondering if she should take early retirement, when Drapkin's phone call pierces the stuffy silence of their apartment. *Her* apartment.

"My wife hasn't eaten in four days," says Drapkin. "You're killing her."

"How did you get my number?" demands Arlene.

"From the home," he answers. "They're concerned about Connie too."

"They had no business giving you my number."

"You're probably right about that," concedes Drapkin. "But they did. Now if we could talk for a few just minutes..."

"As far as I'm concerned," she answers, "we have nothing to talk about."

She hangs up the phone and the conversation ends as rapidly as it starts. This abruptness is so unlike her, she recognizes. She usu-

ally has a difficult time getting rid of fundraisers from the Police
Athletic League and accented men telemarketing aluminum siding, even though she lives in a cooperative apartment. Yet something about Jim Drapkin unnerves her, maybe the instinct that he'll
convince her to do something that runs against her own best judgment. In fact, the doubts set in as soon as she returns the telephone
to its console. Arlene is not by her nature a selfish woman—but
years of marriage to a wayward man have limited the scope of her
generosity, particularly where her husband's favors are concerned.
Still, she believes Drapkin when he says that his wife is suffering. By
the time she has heated up her dinner—the remnants of a chicken
sandwich from the teacher's cafeteria—she knows that the plight
of the judge's wife will prevent her from sleeping.

It's eight o'clock when she fills her gas tank on the Bronx-Yon-
kers border, nine fifteen by the time she pulls into the dark parking lot at the Valhalla Home. Visiting hours have been over for
forty-five minutes, but Arlene knows that the nurses will let her
in. She has an excellent rapport with the staff. Two of the health
aides once worked alongside her late sister-in-law, a geriatric social
worker, at another assisted-living facility, so they afford Benny their
own version of professional courtesy: checking that his dentures
are regularly brushed, that his bed sheets are perpetually fresh. As
fate would have it, Annie Serspinksi herself answers the buzzer
this evening. The nursing director displays no hint of surprise at
Arlene's after-hours appearance—it's as though she has anticipated
the visit—and she merely warns her guest not to slip on the wet
floors as she leads her into the television lounge. Several ancient
women are watching a documentary about penguins, their wheelchairs drawn within arm's length of the TV set, as though huddled
around a fire for warmth. One of the women has a gauze bandage
encircling her jaw. The blind lady is pacing around the coffee table,

the ball of her wrist pressed to her temple, dictating a letter to a young black health aide in a skintight Che Guevara T-shirt. Benny sits alone in the far corner of this madhouse. He taps his fingertips together rhythmically, appearing simultaneously anxious and glum. Connie Drapkin is nowhere to be seen.

"It's me, Arlene," says Arlene. "Your wife."

Arlene squeezes his brittle hand. She leans down and kisses his dry, sunken cheek.

"It's not your turn," Benny answers. "It's *the other Arlene's* turn."

"I know it is," she agrees. "It's her turn too."

She removes a carefully-wrapped napkin from her handbag and offers her husband a *hamantaschen*, but he shakes his head vehemently. And then she hears a sound she hardly recognizes, a soft, high-pitched sob that she hasn't heard in many years. Benny is weeping.

"I want to marry *the other Arlene*," he says, "before it's too late."

"I know you do," Arlene agrees. She dabs his eyes with her kerchief, but cannot bear to hear him bawling over another woman. This time, she understands, it is not his fault; but that doesn't make it any easier.

After a short visit, she returns to the lobby and tells Annie Serspinski what the nursing director already knows. "I can't let the poor woman starve, can I?" she asks.

"Of course, you can't," agrees Annie. "Mrs. Drapkin is a very sweet lady."

"But I don't want them holding hands in the lounge," Arlene adds.

She had a right to some dignity, after all. She has feelings too.

"I'll see what I can do," agrees Annie. That's her way of saying: *Okay, I'll intervene—but with misgivings.* The nursing director pats Arlene on the shoulder and adds, "Dr. Steinhoff is very lucky to have you."

. . . . .

Three days later Benny presents her with a clay ostrich. Each of the bird's tail feathers scrolls into a perfect clef. Usually, Benny crafts his animals in pairs—as though preparing for a flood—but there is only one sculpture on this occasion. They're chatting together in the snack room, because it's the first Saturday of the month and the occupational therapist has commandeered the television lounge for the show-tune festival. Arlene can hear the distant mayhem of elderly voices crooning "I'm Gonna Wash That Man Right Out of My Hair" and "Get Me to the Church on Time." Most of Valhalla's residents are either singing, or away on daytrips with relatives, so the snack room's only other occupant is Connie Drapkin. The dopey woman dozes in front of the refrigerator, her mouth open like a flytrap. A thin film of drool extends down her chin onto her turquoise blouse. When Benny loses focus, which is often, his gaze settles upon his sleeping friend, and he smiles. Arlene also glances at Connie warily, from time to time, but she doesn't dare wheel the woman's chair into the corridor. It crosses her mind that Benny's other ostrich might be in Connie's bedroom, and this makes Arlene want to crush both birds to powder. Of all Connie Drapkin's offenses—stealing her husband's affections, holding his hand—taking the clay ostrich seems to Arlene the cruelest and most personal.

She had already kissed Benny goodbye, and she is pulling on her winter gloves, when Jim Drapkin appears at the door of the snack room. Arlene first catches the judge's reflection in the panes of the toaster oven—his strong chin and thick neck distorted by the contours of the stainless steel. He's probably her own age, far too young and spry to be saddled with a demented woman in her mid-seventies. She feels genuinely bad for him. The judge crosses the linoleum and places his broad palm upon Arlene's shoulder.

"Thank you," he says. "I'm very grateful for what you did."

Arlene stands up. "I didn't have much of a choice."

"You *did* have a choice," replies Drapkin. "Don't think I'm not appreciative."

The judge retrieves her coat and umbrella from the radiator. "You'll get used to it after a few weeks," he says. "I may look okay with this now—as though I don't care—but I cried like a baby the first time I saw them together."

"I suppose people can get used to anything," says Arlene. Sometimes, on the drive north through Westchester, she reflects upon the men and women who survived the Nazi death camps and went on to build rich lives in Israel and America—to raise new families after losing their own. She wonders: *Is that life's final lesson? That there is no bottom, no breaking point.* "There are things," she says, "that I would never *want* to get used to."

"Agreed," says Drapkin.

He accompanies her down the corridor toward the elevators. The chorus of "I Could Have Danced All Night" grows louder as they pass the lounge.

"It's easier not having had children," he observes. "Do you have kids?"

Arlene shakes her head. "Not yet," she answers. That's the same retort she has been serving up since menopause, a way to mask the agony of reproductive misfortune. *But how could anybody find it easier without children? That was the most upsetting part. Even harder than tolerating Connie.*

"I've forced myself to accept this," Drapkin explains. "Your husband and my wife, I mean. But if I had children watching, I don't think I could handle it."

Oh, so that's what he was trying to say, thinks Arlene.

She steps into the elevator. Drapkin follows. Other visitors enter behind them—two women in their forties with matching, wide-set eyes—and the heavy double doors slam closed. "This elevator has a mind of its own," observes one of the women. "Mark my words: One of these days, somebody's going to lose a finger." Arlene does not respond. She examines the glass-encased posters advertising food drives, and blood drives, and something called "The Grandchildren's Carnival," until they arrive at the ground floor. The elevator recoils like a yoyo. Drapkin holds the doors open with his elbow while she exists.

"My wife has always loved knowledge," he says, apropos of nothing. "She was a high school principal. Before that, she taught French and Italian."

"Did she?" asks Arlene.

"Say, will you sit with me in the lobby for a minute?" asks Drapkin. He sounds like a man *trying* to sound casual. "The coffee here isn't half bad."

"Compared to what?"

"Compared to the cafeteria at Presbyterian Hospital for starters," he replies.

That's the right thing for Drapkin to say, the one angle that might persuade her to join him for a respite. She recognizes how easily she could allow herself to bond with this man over their mutual suffering. But to what end? The suffering would still be there, like a sack of boulders piled on her tired spine. Besides, she does not like driving home after dark.

"So what do you think? A quick cup of joe?"

"I really can't. Not today," Arlene apologizes. "Maybe another time."

"Okay, sure. But I wanted to ask you one more thing. You're going to think this is a crazy idea at first, but please don't reject it straight out." He takes a deep breath and looks at his shoes. Arlene fears the man may invite her on a more formal date. Instead, he asks, "How would you feel if we let them have a wedding?"

Arlene thinks she has heard him wrong. Or mistaken his meaning again.

"Not a real wedding. Nothing legal or binding," continues Drapkin. "But I have a close friend who's a rabbi. Reconstructionist. He'd be glad to come over next Sunday and perform a service for them. . . . We could think of it as a commitment ceremony."

"You can't be serious?"

"Why not? What harm will it do?" asks Drapkin. He sounds self-assured now, incandescent, as though selling her an appliance or a fringe religion. "Connie keeps asking me. Apparently, your husband proposes every time he sees her. Please, Arlene. You have an opportunity to make two wonderful people extremely happy . . ."

Arlene knows she should run or scream. This is pure insanity. She's given this man an inch and now he's taken half the planet. But she's so worn down these days, so desperate, that there's something appealing about buckling to this stranger's madness.

"Trust me," he says. "Now can I tell Miss Serspinski that I have your okay?"

"I honestly don't know what to say," she says. "I'm overwhelmed."

"You don't have to say a word," he answers. He holds his index finger up to his lips. "Have some faith in me and I'll take care of everything."

The judge reaches for her arm and squeezes her wrist in both his hands—like a schoolboy offering a shy hug at the end of a dance. Then he darts through the elevator doors, before she has a chance to reject his mad plan, leaving her alone in the lobby.

. . . . .

Arlene has all week long to thwart Drapkin's lunacy—to call Annie Serspinki and expressly disapprove of the sham marriage—but she doesn't. She gets as far as copying the judge's number off her caller ID, thinking she might speak with him directly, but she's no longer confident that her nerves can handle the confrontation. Tomorrow, she tells herself. She'll call on Tuesday, then Wednesday. She keeps drawing lines in the sand, as she once did when she tried to quit smoking, but instead of phoning Connie's husband, she elevates her feet on Benny's threadbare Barcalounger and smokes a cigarette. On Saturday, she decides, she will challenge Jim Drapkin face-to-face. Who cares if it's short notice? How difficult can it be to cancel a mock wedding ceremony at a nursing home? But it rains heavily over Friday night, a nor'easter that devours the last of the snow, and she hears on the radio that the parkways have washed out all along the Hudson. Later, she has trouble starting her car and has to phone the Automobile Association to jumpstart her battery. By the time she's ready for the seventy-five minute drive, it's already one o'clock—and what's the point, really, of arriving so late in the afternoon? Better to conserve her energies for the following day. That's the key to caring for the chronically incapacitated: pacing oneself. So for the first time in nearly twenty months, Arlene calls her husband and tells him she won't be able to visit. *Ever?* he asks. And then somehow, inexplicably, it is Sunday morning—a bright Sunday morning in early March. She packs a thick slice of home-baked marble cake for Benny's desert, and a tuna salad for her own lunch, as she does every Sunday. Outside, chickadees and nuthatches flitter through the budding crabapples. The highway medians are alive with crocuses, steam rising off the asphalt.

The drive is painstaking. Traffic narrows to one lane in several places, orange cones and state cruisers cordoning off pockets of floodwater. Arlene worries that her driving days are numbered. And then how will she visit Benny? She makes a mental note to check out bus routes between the Bronx and Westchester.

Jim Drapkin greets her in the lobby as she signs the visitor's log. He's wearing a brown jacket with oversized lapels and too broad a tie. His companion, Rabbi Pastarnack, is a rotund man in this twenties or thirties. Far too young, she thinks, to be a rabbi.

"I'm so glad you're here," says Drapkin. He makes her presence sound incidental—as though he'd have married Benny off without her. "When I didn't see you yesterday, I thought you might not come at all."

"Well, I did," she says.

"I've chosen several psalms that seem to fit the occasion," interjects the rabbi. His high voice grates like a squeaky hinge. "There won't be seven blessings, you understand, because it's not a valid marriage under Jewish law, but your husband is welcome to break a glass."

"Miss Serspinki gave me a light bulb," says Drapkin. "That should work."

She should stop this, Arlene knows. She should pull the plug on this twisted plan before it does any permanent damage. But she's so tired of making decisions, of fighting battles, of arguing with hospitals and insurance companies. How easy it is to let Jim Drapkin steer her into the elevator while he speaks about the importance of being "forward-looking." The elevator opens on the second floor of the home and a girl in white baking fatigues wheels the wedding cake into the elevator. *Benny & Connie* in chocolate frosting. "I still have the little plastic figurines from our wedding," she says. She is not sure why she says this. How can she possibly connect her formal summer wedding at the Plaza with this dismal spectacle?

"You should have brought them along," says Drapkin.

"Maybe next time," Arlene answers. How stupid. But he doesn't seem to notice.

The television lounge is decked out in paper streamers. Folding chairs have been arranged on either side of a narrow aisle. A portable lectern rests atop the television set. Arlene can't help

wondering who possesses the remote control—if some old gee-
zer won't click on one of the Sunday talk shows at the height of
the ceremony. She squeezes into one of the back rows, beside the
woman with the jaw bandage. She does not want Benny to see
her—she is afraid to see him—but Jim Drapkin beckons her to
move up front. "Aren't you going to accompany your husband up
the aisle?" he asks. So, reluctantly, Arlene advances toward the front
of the crowded lounge. Annie Serspinski winks at her from a perch
on the radiator. Benny looks up from his wheelchair, as she settles
down beside him. "I know you," he says.

Then Jim Drapkin presses play on the portable stereo and the
room fills with Dorothy Lamour crooning, "It Had To Be You."
The retired judge had certainly done his research; this is Benny's
favorite recording. Several of the demented women in the second
row sing along, as though they're attending occupational therapy.
Suddenly, Arlene finds herself on her feet, a roomful of aging eyes
upon her, steering Benny's wheelchair toward the lectern. She
stops beside the television set and adjusts his bow tie. At the same
moment, Jim Drapkin disappears into the neighboring room—the
patients' library—and he returns seconds later, pushing his wife
before him. The retired judge smiles at Arlene, but she looks away.
Beyond the bay windows, squirrels are nibbling birdseed from the
hanging feeders.

"Good morning," says Rabbi Pastarnack. "God bless you all."

Jim Drapkin is still watching her. Arlene can see him at the corner of her eye. His handsome cheer is like a magnet. She lets her
gaze meet his and, sheepishly, she smiles back.

What follows reminds Arlene of some primitive ritual—one
of those symbolic ceremonies that anthropologists record in the
corners of sub-Saharan Africa and Polynesia. It's a *National Geo-
graphic* caption: "Spouses handing over their demented partners."

She cannot focus on the psalms. Instead, she finds herself thinking of her own wedding, of how ravishing Benny looked in the Italian tuxedo he'd borrowed from his uncle. She'd known then that he was a ladies' man, all thrill and machismo, but she'd thought she might tame him. And she has—*in a way*. Or time has done the taming, maybe, and she's come along for the ride. She can still see the dazzling chandeliers of the grand ballroom at the Plaza, she can smell the lilacs in her corsage and sense the champagne rising into her temples. Arlene is sobbing, her heart brimming with thirty-seven-year-old anticipation, when Benny's voice jolts her back to the present.

"I do," he says.

Two words. Not even a sentence. But once again, her world is changed forever.

"I do," answers Connie.

That's the cue for Jim Drapkin to place the velvet bag containing the light bulb at the base of Benny's wheelchair. He urges the groom to wheel forward—and the glass shatters, cementing the union. Rabbi Pastarnack pronounces the couple to be "bound in love."

The lovebirds do not kiss or speak. They merely smile at each other, benighted. Arlene can't help thinking they are suited for each other now, that they speak a language as foreign to her as Aramaic or Swahili. She steps around her husband's wheelchair and plants her lips on Benny's leathery forehead. She can learn to share. What choice does she have? But then Benny begins coughing, a deep fitful wheeze from the depths of his throat. His face turns red, white. His breathing grows so strained that the nursing staff phones the doctor-on-call. This is not death. Only a reminder that death has taken note of Benny. By evening, Arlene's husband can sit up in bed while she feeds him a slice of the wedding cake.

He does not ask after his new bride. Instead, he grins like a cookie thief and asks whose birthday they are celebrating.

·····

Visiting hours have been over for hours when Arlene finally bids goodbye to Benny. To her surprise, Jim Drapkin is waiting for her in the lobby. The judge is seated opposite the panoramic fish tank, spying on the gouramis, his plaid cap balanced on his knee. He stands up as soon as he sees her—a true gentleman. It strikes Arlene that he is "family" now, in a strange way, although the bounds of this arrangement remain untested.

"Are you okay?" he asks.

Arlene nods. She *is* okay. She is adjusting to being okay.

Drapkin looks relieved. "I wasn't sure you'd let me go through with this," he says. "Honestly, I thought you'd stop me."

"So did I."

Arlene doesn't know what else to say, so she says nothing. She is amazed at how comfortable she feels now in the presence of this kind, eccentric man who has so rapidly inserted himself into her life. He adjusts his cap to the contours of his head. Then he steps toward her, pensive, probing, as though he might take her in his arms. This is their moment. Behind him, the gouramis continue their concentric pilgrimage. But instead of embracing her, Drapkin asks, "How about you? Do you think you'll ever get remarried?"

It's not an idle question. Idle questions are not the judge's style. It's not a proposal either, of course, but Arlene senses it could be a prelude. If she were willing. Soon enough—maybe months, maybe years—she could be Connie's successor. She considers answering yes, that she might remarry someday, although she knows that's a wishful lie: Once Benny no longer needs her, she'll wander the sidewalks of Riverdale alone. So even as Arlene lets this lovely, handsome man escort her out of the Valhalla Home on his sturdy arm, she sees that the future will separate them rather than unite them—that this day is the closest to each other that they will ever come. By the morning, Jim Drakpin will be moving forward again, while she will remain glacially frozen. The fissure between them will open up, day after day, as vast as the distance between life and death.

Amazing Things Are Happening Here

· ·

We were short one lunatic.

I know it's entirely out-of-bounds to refer to our patients as lunatics, and I generally don't, but it's also not every night that Bernadette does a head count and comes up one head short. Fact is, it hasn't happened before in my seventeen years as charge nurse, which is as good as never as far as I'm concerned. Sure, we've had agoraphobics who've hidden under beds, and once a detox patient dozed off inside an electric dryer, but all it takes is a careful search and we find them. There's just not much place to lose oneself on a psych ward. When I first started here at the VA hospital in Laurenville—back when male nurses stood out like drag queens and most of our vets were straight off transports from the Gulf—doddering Miss K was the charge nurse on the graveyard shift, and she'd get the census wrong as often as not, but Bernadette is studying to be an NP, and she's the queen of arithmetic. If she says we're missing a nutcase, we're missing a nutcase. Time to dispatch the paddy wagons and the giant butterfly nets—or, in the language of the Veterans' Administration, to implement Code White.

We *don't* implement Code White, of course. That's how people get fired. A guy can have a perfect record for seventeen years— never so much as drop an order or misplace a syringe—but suddenly a patient goes AWOL, even for only a few hours, and the bigwigs in Washington will be clamoring for somebody's scalp. Far better to let things blow over, to wait for the missing loony-tune to reappear. No point in risking your pension because some troublemaker has bested you at hide-and-seek.

"So who are we looking for?" I asked.

"Dunham," said Bernadette.

"Dunham?"

Bernadette displayed the palms of her enormous hands—her way of announcing that she knew little more about the business than I did. She's a busty, copper-skinned girl from South Carolina, all eyes and teeth, the sort of creature that a forty-eight year old bachelor could easily make a fool of himself over, if he weren't careful, but the skirt-chasing chapter in my life was long closed.

"He'll have come in yesterday," she said. "On the second shift. All it says in the chart is 'uncooperative, hold over for further evaluation.'"

"Black? White?" I asked. "Tall? Short? Bald?"

"Can't be helping you there." Bernadette adjusted the computer monitor so that I might watch as she scrolled through Dunham's electronic admission note; none of the blanks on the template had been completed. "Another masterpiece from Dr. Thorough," she quipped. "Don't let all of the data overwhelm you."

Dr. Thorough and Dr. Brilliant were Bernadette's nicknames for the two attending physicians on the unit. Thorough, whose Slavic surname was longer than a freight train, had cut his medical teeth running a charity hospital in Belgrade. Brilliant, whose real name was short, and Turkish, and uncannily deficient in vowels, stood only one year from retirement and had the taxing habit of leaving his door keys in locks. Neither was particularly invested in his job, or popular with the patients, but they were both easy to manage from below, which is what really mattered. Before Dr. Thorough, we'd briefly had a unit chief fresh out of training at Yale, a bright-eyed girl who viewed inpatient psychiatry as her "life's calling"—and we scrambled through hell and back to keep her from making a royal mess of the place. As far as Dr. Thorough was concerned, anything that afforded him more time to breed Cairn Terriers or to parasail qualified as first-rate healthcare. In contrast, Dr. Brilliant's management style consisted entirely of consulting specialists in other fields and of relating anecdotes about his twin granddaughters.

It was already after six a.m.—nearly medication time. And then the dynamic duo of Brilliant and Thorough would arrive at eight o'clock for morning rounds. I ushered Bernadette into the break room where Hyacinth—the senior swing nurse—sat watching a Mexican game show and snacking on sardines. Hyacinth is the real deal: six step-children at home and a voice strong enough to dislodge shingles. I swear the place smelled like the Creve Coeur Fish Market in August.

"Dunham is missing," I announced, "but you can't tell anyone."

"Who the hell is Dunham?" asked Hyacinth.

"He came in yesterday, second shift," I said. "Seems he didn't stay long."

Hyacinth plucked a tiny bone from her teeth. "What is *that* supposed to mean?"

"It means he's missing. Unaccounted for. On the lam."

"Whatever. He's probably napping in one of the washing machines."

I sensed lava mounting in my temples. "I'm telling you he's gone."

"Okay. He's gone. Did you call a Code White?"

"Like hell I did," I snapped. "I'm not giving up my paycheck that easy."

Our eyes met. My stomach quivered—as though I were staring down a grizzly bear brandishing a chainsaw.

"So what now?" interjected Bernadette.

"Now we pretend as though nothing is wrong," I explained—hatching my plan in the moment. "There are three of us. As long as one of us is working each shift, nobody needs to know that Dunham isn't here. He's bound to turn up eventually."

Hyacinth looked as though she'd swallowed a sardine stuffed with glass shards.

"You're crazy, man," she said. "We could go to jail."

I nodded. "Yeah, we could. Or we could get canned. . . . Any better ideas?"

Hyacinth rocked her head back and forth slowly, her nostrils flaring, as she weighed my proposal. A woman on the television screen spun a glistening vertical wheel and the audience applauded. In the corridor, Abe Shimmelbach, one of our paranoid schizophrenics, chanted his morning prayers.

"Besides," I said, grinning. "Amazing things are happening here."

That's the Laurenville VA's motto: *Amazing Things Are Happening Here*. It was entered into a contest for the hospital's fiftieth anniversary, and they've got it hanging from banners in the lobby. Funny thing is, it's not even original—the employee who submitted the slogan pinched it from a hospital in New York City—but by the time the brass on the ninth floor caught on, they'd already paid for the signs.

"You two can handle all the meds today," I ordered. "And record Mr. Dunham's as 'refused by patient.'"

Hyacinth's face blazed with consternation, her eyes bulging beneath her hand-penciled brows. "And what will *you* be doing while we do your job?"

"I'll be in morning rounds, Miss Pike," I said. "Somebody has to account for what Mr. Dunham's been up to while he's not here."

· · · · ·

The powers-that-be had decided to renovate the conference room, so morning rounds took place off the unit—in a window-less space that doubled as an overflow storeroom for the ortho-pedics division. Assorted braces and collars poked out of crates stacked along the far wall. On the shelf above the busted sink, a row of fiberglass prosthetic feet—some dating from the Eisen-hower era—stood at macabre attention. We cleared the plastic-wrapped crutches from the table every morning, then returned the following day to discover yet more crutches, as though the aluminum appendages sprouted overnight like squid tentacles. From next door, the sounds of the men's lavatory drifted through the air shaft, leaving nothing to the imagination.

Dr. Brilliant arrived ten minutes late and informed us that Dr. Thorough had phoned in sick—but that we had a new third-year medical student with us that morning, Zachary, who'd be able to pick up the slack. Then our venerated leader asked me to read from the overnight log book. Vicky, who'd doubled as both charge nurse on the early shift *and* acting nurse manager ever since Miss Denton had fallen off her bicycle, was more than happy to sport me overtime to share in her duties. So I read aloud. Each patient report—Shimmelbach, Marcus, Frotherberg—brought us closer to Dunham.

"Dunham," I announced. "Refusing meds. Otherwise calm and cooperative."

"Vital signs?" inquired Dr. Brilliant.

I invented the numbers as I spoke, rendering him stable but slightly hypertensive.

"I didn't have much opportunity to speak with Mr. Dunham yesterday," observed Dr. Brilliant. "Why don't we make him a project for our esteemed medical student? Let's say we'll interview him together around noon..."

I could feel the chill of Code White enveloping me—the countless investigative hearings and rehearings, the interviews with successive grievance officers, then the cash-strapped months spent mailing out résumés to nursing homes and prisons.

"Noon is lunchtime," I ventured. I drew a deep breath and added, "Dunham could use the calories..."

"An excellent point, that!" declared Dr. Brilliant—holding up his index finger like a medieval rabbi or a television detective. He extended his arm suddenly, as though in accusation, fixing his finger on the hapless medical student. "Why don't you interview him on your own, Zachary? And then we can discuss the case afterwards."

"Sure," agreed Zachary. He was a handsome, clean-cut kid—his white coat as stiff as chain-mail. "Could you spell that name for me?"

I spelled Dunham's name. "First name Edward."

"Edward," echoed the medical student.

And then an impulse seized hold of me—perhaps clever, possibly destructive—and I added, "But he goes by Ward."

"Ward Dunham," said Dr. Brilliant. "You'll have to find out *why* he goes by Ward and not Ed," he instructed the student. "Names are often the most revealing signs of pathology. Sometimes, a nickname tells you your entire diagnosis. If a fellow comes in and his wife calls him Dickie or Little Peter, that might be all you need to know."

Zachary's face colored. Ms. Hernandez, our temporary social worker, started cleaning her spectacles with a tissue.

"Dunham is one of our regular customers," I lied—glad that most of the day staff had turned over since Dr. Yale's departure. "He comes in depressed, keeps to himself, returns home after a few weeks." I looked pointedly at Zachary. "The man is quiet as a shadow. You'll hardly even know he's here."

. . . . .

Now I was neck deep in Ribbon Creek, as the expression goes, and the hardest part of the battle was yet to come. To be honest—maybe because I was running on a sleep deficit—my adrenaline surged. As much as getting caught scared the bejeezus out of me, fabricating Dunham's data—and pulling it off so effortlessly—was about as much fun as anything I'd done in years. I made a point of positioning myself at the nurses' station, playing checkers with a one-eyed sociopath named O'Grigg, anticipating the moment when Zachary would come in search of his first patient. Sure enough, not half an hour elapsed before the kid appeared, his high-tech stethoscope draped over his broad shoulders, clipboard tucked under his elbow like a track coach.

"I'm looking for Mr. Dunham," he announced.

"Dunham . . . Dunham," I repeated—as though I attached no particular importance to the name. "Did you check his room?"

The kid looked at me like I had asked him to mine salt. "Not yet," he said.

"That's where I'd start, doc," I suggested. "Dunham's a late sleeper. Tell you what, though, if you give me a second, I'll go with you." To Jimmy O'Grigg, I said, "I'll be back in five. Don't cheat." Then I steered Zachary toward the four-person room that—since we're always under-census during the summer months—Mr. Dunham allegedly shared with three empty cots.

"You becoming a psychiatrist, doc?"

I make a point of calling the med students "doc" because it sounds deferential—and as a nurse, if you *sound* obsequious enough, you can run the show.

"Nope," he answered—almost defensive. "I'm going into neurosurgery. . . . Not that there's anything wrong with psychiatry, it's just . . ."

"Not your cup of Haldol?"

"That's right," he agreed. "Not my cup of Haldol."

I had already pegged the kid for a future surgeon—you could sense it in his bearing, which conveyed an air of self-certainty. I suppose if he'd actually planned on becoming a headshrinker, we'd all have been screwed. But he was more than willing to let me lead the search for Dunham, as I'd anticipated, and I even made a show of checking inside the closets.

"Looks like Dunham hasn't changed one bit," I said. I lowered my voice, as though letting the kid in on a secret. "Dunham's a hider," I revealed. "He'll climb into any available bed and doze off until the owner returns to toss him out. Honestly, he enjoys the attention." I stole a rapid glance up the corridor to ascertain that none of the other patients was in earshot. "If you want to save yourself a lot of effort, just tell the attending that Dunham seems down and could use a stronger anti-depressant."

Zachary flashed me a look that screamed: *You're not a goddam doctor. What the flying fuck do you know?* I've never regretted becoming a nurse—it's a good job for a recovered drunk who can't stand office work—but if I'd known how often I'd get that look, I might have followed my brothers into the gutter-and-tile business. A guy like Zachary is going to treat OR nurses like dog shit someday, but if his roof ever springs a leak, he'll be down on his Brooks-Brothers-swaddled suburban knees, begging for mercy. I could practically hear his mind ticking as he ran his mental paws over the corners of my idea, weighing whether it was worth the risk to avoid the labor. One meaty hand jangled the coins in the pocket of his slacks.

He lowered his voice to match mine. "You sure it's okay?"

"Trust me, doc." I draped an arm around the kid's shoulders and maneuvered him toward his workstation. "The less you have to do with Dunham, the better. He *bit* the last medical student who tried to interview him. Did I mention that? And he's got hepatitis too." I patted the kid's arm in macho affection. "Leave it to me. You let Nurse Carlo manage Dunham, doc, and you'll get your 'High Honors' in psychiatry."

"If you're positive it's best for the patient," said Zachary—latching onto every medical student's failsafe excuse.

"Positive, doc," I replied. "What Dunham needs is peace and tranquility. I know the man better than I know myself." I was high on life at that moment—as high as I'd ever been on the hooch at my worst. "He's a tall, lanky fellow. Long face, dark hair. Keloid scar shaped like a croissant on his left cheek," I added. "In case anybody asks."

· · · · ·

I'll confess that, ever since Papa convinced me that I could grow macaroni from a noodle sprig planted in tomato sauce, I'd been fascinated by schemes and hoaxes: The Great Train Robbery, Cold War espionage, Orson Welles broadcasting "The War of the Worlds." Never did I dream that I would be part of such a plot. After two days, however, it became clear that the game was playing out in our favor. None of my practical concerns ever materialized: Dunham's relatives—if he had any—didn't come to visit him or phone to ask after his condition. No agents from the city marshal's office showed up to serve the man with a restraining order or a bench warrant. In fact, the only person who ever noticed he'd gone missing was Meltz, one of the OCD patients, who obsessively counted the meal trays in the dining hall. This matter did require some finesse: First, explaining to Meltz that Dunham had recently been diagnosed with esophageal cancer, and so could only take his nutrients intravenously, then sneaking onto Dr. Brilliant's computer after he forgot to log out and canceling the patient's diet order. That was the last time I harbored any doubts. By day three, *not* concealing Dunham's absence would have seemed abnormal.

Don't get me wrong: I was not oblivious to the ethical considerations. Mr. Dunham could have been stuck somewhere inside a ventilation duct, tapping S-O-S on the plumbing in Morse code, or ensconced behind a heavy bureau. Unit 4B is supposedly idiot-proof—but let's face it, our patients can be virtuosos at idiocy. The possibility also crossed my mind that Dunham might be wandering the streets, armed with a copy of Dr. Brilliant's keys, planning to shove an innocent bystander into moving traffic. I won't make any excuses for myself. I knew there were risks. But the way I saw it, it wasn't my fault that Dunham had vanished, and I didn't owe it to anyone to play the scapegoat. If you want nurses to call Code White when a patient disappears, don't cut off their goddam balls for doing it. Besides, mental health is no exact science. Half the patients we discharge from this place are still *some* threat to the public—you can't keep shelling out the taxpayers' dollars indefinitely—but nobody castrates Brilliant or Thorough for that.

On the third morning of Dunham's "stay," Dr. Thorough announced that he'd be taking his terriers to a conformation show in Creve Coeur, and Dr. Brilliant would be covering for him through the end of the week. So the next day, Brilliant arrived early, hoping to complete all of his notes before rounds. When I unlocked the orthopedics room at seven fifty, I found him seated at the head of the table, munching pickles from the jar.

"Say, Carlo. What's the story with Dunham?"

"Dunham?" I tried to sound calm. "You know how it is with Dunham . . ."

Dr. Brilliant offered me a pickle. I shook my head.

"I couldn't find him this morning," said the psychiatrist. "I'd been hoping to get all these darn notes finished. Not that anybody ever checks, mind you—but now that I'm in charge of the place, I felt it was my responsibility. . . . And no sign of Dunham. I even looked in the washers and dryers for the man. I swear that he's not on the floor."

Brilliant's fingers picked at the paper label on the pickle jar. Dunham meant nothing to him—just another daily note, another obstacle between his breakfast and retirement. The wise approach would have been to come clean: to plead temporary insanity, to stand on my seventeen years of spotless service.

I could have sworn Brilliant's eyes were focused entirely on the jar until he said, "You look anxious, Carlo. Is there something that I should know about Mr. Dunham?"

"I'd completely forgotten," I stammered. "The other night—not last night, but the night before—Dunham was coughing, so the on-call resident ordered him a chest x-ray. You know how the overnight residents can be. . . . Anyway, radiology never called for him— to be blunt, it fell through the cracks—and then, around seven this morning, someone in imaging *finally* put the order through, so we sent him down to take a picture." I shrugged. "Dunham's absolutely fine, probably healthier than either of us. All the man needed was a throat lozenge." Dr. Brilliant's face remained impassive, so I added, "Ward Dunham is a professional complainer, a malcontent. He knows the more he gripes, the longer he stays. . . . But I'm sorry I didn't tell you . . ."

Brilliant's sharp features hardened: I suspect this was what Lenin might have looked like had he survived long enough for his moustache to go gray. The shrink pounded the tabletop and demanded: "Do you know what that is an example of?"

I didn't have time to apologize for my feigned mistake.

"Prioritizing," declared the psychiatrist—his lips curving into a smile. "You have chosen to tell me important things, not to burden me with trivia. Excellent work! Will the world end if I don't know that Dunham had an x-ray? I think not!" Again, Dr. Brilliant pounded the table, and a deep laugh erupted from his belly.

The headshrinker was still chuckling when Zachary entered.

"Am I interrupting?" asked the kid.

"Not at all, doc," I replied—slowly recovering my composure, but with an icy sweat still lacquered across my forearms and neck. "I was just about to mention what a great job you've been doing with Ward Dunham. I haven't seen that guy looking so cheerful in years. Practically good as new. But if you don't mind me throwing in my two cents, I think he could use something for the nightmares . . ."

"Dunham is having nightmares?" asked Dr. Brilliant.

"Once or twice," spluttered Zachary. "He only just mentioned it . . ."

"Prazosin. 1 mg QHS," ordered Dr. Brilliant. "And follow up on his chest x-ray. If I'm going to write a note on the man without seeing him, I don't want to find out next month that he had fulminant tuberculosis."

The psychiatrist twisted open his jar and forced a pickle on the kid.

"Where do all of these crutches keep coming from?" Dr. Brilliant asked the air. "That's your next assignment, Zachary. Now that you've nearly cured Dunham, see if you can read up on spontaneously-generating crutches. It's a pandemic, I tell you. If only we could generate gray matter the way the orthopods grow hardware..."

Poor Zachary looked puzzled to the point of agony; I genuinely felt bad for him.

"He's joking, doc," I whispered. "Just smile and pretend it's funny."

. . . . .

That Friday—at the stroke of midnight—I surprised Bernadette in the break room with a bottle of champagne. I'd sworn off women ever since a gal that I'd been casually dating had tried to pin a cooked-up paternity rap on me, but in light of my success with Dunham, I was starting to reconsider my vows. Besides, the girl looked radiant.

"I'm not going to drink any myself," I explained quickly, removing a crystal flute from my knapsack, "but I wanted to hear the sound of the cork popping. Of course, if *you* indulge in a sip or two, it certainly won't appear in my morning report."

I unfolded a cloth napkin and set it before Bernadette, placing the champagne flute atop the cloth with a flourish.

"Snakes alive, Carlo!" she cried. "What are we celebrating?"

"Our one-week anniversary."

The girl's full lips pursed into a frozen kiss of utter bewilderment.

"You and me and Dunham," I explained. "And Hyacinth too, I suppose. We've gone a full week and nobody has caught on."

Bernadette's mouth relaxed. I decanted champagne into her flute, only a taste at first, but when she made no effort to stop me, I topped off the glass. I suppose tippling on the job was the least of her worries. After I'd stashed the bubbly bottle back in my bag, I snapped open a can of Diet Coke and proposed a toast.

"To Dunham!" I declared. "The ideal patient."

"You really are too much," said Bernadette—and she sipped the champagne.

"So what do you say? Am I a genius or am I a genius?"

"You certainly are *something*," answered Bernadette. Her cheeks glowed under the collective influence of alcohol and fluorescent light. It takes only a few minutes with a girl like that to get a man thinking about all he's missed out on in life. "I figured either Dunham would turn up," she observed, "Or we'd get caught."

"So you *are* impressed?"

"I heard you making recommendations to that student," she said—now sampling the champagne more freely. "You sure to heavens sounded like an MD. Our very own Doctor Carlo. Where did you learn all that about meds?"

"You know how it is," I said—grateful that my complexion was too dark to blush. "You pick stuff up. It's like those pharmacology professors you find in nursing school who sound like they know everything. But it's not because they're really so smart. It's that they teach the same thing, over and over again, so it *sounds* like they're smart."

I refilled Bernadette's glass. "I shouldn't," Bernadette protested—but she did.

For seventeen years, I'd played by the rules, kept to the straight and narrow. Suddenly, I realized how close I'd been to paradise that entire time, so near I could unlock its gates with a round of champagne.

"About Dunham," she said. "I've been meaning to talk to you. I can't keep covering these afternoon shifts."

"It's easy money," I reminded her, rubbing my thumb against my fingertips.

"I know, I know," agreed Bernadette. "But here's the thing. My boyfriend is giving me hell for it—honestly, he thinks I'm cheating on him."

So much for paradise! It is truly amazing how one short word—
boyfriend—can instantly douse a man's spirits. If Bernadette had a
boyfriend, why hadn't she ever mentioned him before? Not that
her private life was any of my business—after all, I didn't go around
telling folks I was an ex-drunk. Still, I felt betrayed.

"What I'm asking," continued Bernadette, "is, what now?
Because we can't keep covering three shifts a day forever."

"Not *forever*," I promised. "A few more weeks. A month, tops. I
just want to switch Dunham's meds around a couple of times . . ."

"Jesus, Carlo. You're really getting off on this, aren't you?"

"So?"

"So, I have to be home for dinner," insisted Bernadette. "I have a
life to lead. Can't you get your rocks off hiding a different patient?"

"Please, Bernadette. Two more weeks." I placed my hand over
hers and looked her square in the eyes. "Dunham is a once in a
lifetime opportunity."

"An opportunity for what?"

An opportunity for what?! That was exactly the sort of infuriating
question a woman would just *have* to ask—the sort of question
that both misses the point and kills all the pleasure in the process.
I felt a sudden relief that Bernadette had a boyfriend, that she was
some other jerk's problem and not mine. "Two more weeks. It's
non-negotiable," I said. "We're not discharging Dunham until he's
good and ready."

. . . . .

The next morning marked the high point of my stint as Dunham's doctor. I convinced Dr. Brilliant to augment his antidepres-
sant with a second-generation antipsychotic, and I'd thrown in a
low-dose anxiolytic for good measure. By the time I was through
with him, the guy was practically a walking pharmacy. And then,

during rounds, I spun this truly inspired tale about how Mrs. Dunham had come to visit—the mother, not the wife—and how the pair had patched up their differences. In my fable, Mrs. Dunham, who was pushing seventy and had recently lost her third husband, brought along a home-cooked lamb stew. I couldn't resist offering Dr. Thorough the leftovers for his dogs, knowing full-well that the animals consumed an all-organic diet of specially-bred meats imported from Canada. At the end of my Oscar-worthy narrative, Zachary chimed in that he'd stayed late the prior evening, and that he'd had a "long talk" with Mrs. Dunham—enlightening us that she'd worked as a children's librarian. "On a cruise ship," I added. "A children's librarian *on a cruise ship*."

The taste of victory was still fresh on my palate, and I was catnapping on the sofa in the break room, when Hyacinth showed up for her swing shift. She hunkered down at the folding table and turned on the television. It was only a matter of seconds before the stench of canned fish reached toxic levels. I tried to fall asleep while breathing through my mouth, then reluctantly wiped the haze from my eyes.

"Oh, Miss Pike," I said, my voice dripping with mock-surprise. "I didn't realize you were here."

"You don't own the break room," she shot back.

That's when I nearly lost it: When it struck me—only for an instant—that it might be worth losing my pension if Hyacinth lost hers too. But I'd been at this job long enough to know that indifference was the best revenge. If some dimwitted battle-axe with an attitude rubs her stinking sardines in your nose, just pick up your ass and move on. I was already at the door—my hand on the knob—when Hyacinth spoke.

"We've got a problem," she said.

"What sort of problem?"

"I'm taking my vacation next week," she said. "So you better finish your funny business with Dunham before then."

"You couldn't have told me this sooner?"

"I didn't know *sooner*," she snapped. "And it's not *my* job to tell *you* anything."

I returned to the sofa. On the television, a rotund meteorologist was predicting violent squalls along the seaboard. Someone had left a plastic bag atop the refrigerator—a flagrant violation of the unit's anti-suicide precautions—and for a fleeting moment, I fantasized that I might arrange for Dunham to suffocate himself. After all, he'd gone through too much already to depart as a run-of-the-mill discharge.

"Be reasonable, Miss Pike," I said. "We'll figure this out."

"There's nothing to figure out. I'm done with this bullshit. Period." Hyacinth wrapped the remains of her lunch in wax-paper. "I had nothing to do with this guy disappearing, and I want nothing to do with covering it up."

"It's too late for that. Come on. We're all in this together."

"I'm not *in* anything." She stood up. "Now I have a job to do..."

"I don't have the energy for this, Miss Pike. You're going to postpone your vacation, okay? There's no way I can get Dunham out of here by next week."

We stood face to face. I'd never realized Hyacinth's height until that moment.

"I won't do it," she threatened. "Do not test me."

"You *will* do it, Miss Pike," I said—not breaking my gaze. "Do you know why? Because if you don't do it, I'll claim this was all your idea. And so will Bernadette. *You* let Dunham escape and then *you* pleaded with us to cover for you." I leaned forward—my nose only inches from Hyacinth's chin. "So you postpone that fucking vacation of yours. Am I making myself clear? Or else you'd better start asking yourself how those step-brats of yours are going to feel when they visit their Mama in the slammer."

I didn't wait for a reply. Instead, I flipped off the television and found myself an empty couch in the day room, where I dozed off to Shimmelbach praying in Hebrew.

· · · · ·

That night I decided that Mr. Dunham was due for a setback. Nothing fatal—just a tearful episode, or maybe a panic attack. I also considered accusing him of smoking in the bathroom—but I was apprehensive, fearful that Vicky, if she caught word of the infraction, might take the matter up with the offender during the dayshift. Instead, I decided that Dunham's sister would phone from Alaska. She had just given birth to triplets—Faith, Hope and Charity—and he'd be named godfather *in absentia*. Of course, as always happened when I was in a hurry to get to rounds, some whackjob chose that moment to go berserk: In this case it was Arcaya, our resident sex fiend, cornering a female janitor in the linen alcove. By the time I'd loaded him with a double dose of IM thorazine, Dr. Brilliant was lecturing Zachary on the mating habits of crutches.

"Sorry, I'm late," I apologized.

"You are not late. You are early for tomorrow," declared Dr. Brilliant. "I was about to congratulate our esteemed colleague here on the wonderful job he's done with Mr. Dunham. Excellent work!"

"Thank you," said Zachary.

"About Dunham—," I ventured.

Dr. Brilliant cut me off. "We *all* deserve credit, of course. The nurses too. Miss Pike tells me that he's completely recovered. Better than new. If you'll take care of the paperwork, Zachary, we'll get him out of here this morning."

"That's the thing," I objected. "He's not ready."

"Not ready? They're *never* ready," said the headshrinker. "What did you call him, Carlo? A professional complainer? A malcontent? But we can't keep the man forever. This isn't the Plaza Hotel. This isn't Club Med. The man is cured and it's time for him to leave."

"But Dunham said—"

"Enough of Dunham," ordered the shrink. "If there's one thing I have no patience for, it's malingering. Get him out of here, Zachary. *Today!*"

Somehow I read through the overnight logbook that morning, and scribbled down the physicians' orders, but I don't remember it. All I recall is the searing loss that I experienced as Zachary typed up Dunham's discharge orders, and then the pain of watching my patient's shadow pass one last time through those locked double-doors—followed by the permanent ache of knowing that Ward Dunham remains out there, somewhere: forever beckoning, always beyond my reach.

Dyads

· · · · · · · · · ·

The whales arrive in Rhode Island on Take Your Daughter to Work Day, but Wally and I don't have any daughters—no children at all. Victor Navarre, on the other hand, has a seven-year-old beauty named Patagonia, who is accompanying him out to the field station. The girl sits in the prow of the patrol boat, bundled into a life jacket that extends past her knees, peppering her father with wonderfully haphazard questions: *What's an albatross? What's an abortion? When lighting strikes the ocean, why doesn't it kill all the fish?* Every so often, she points to a distant slab of rock and asks: Is *that one* a seal? Hooded seals are the subject of Dr. Navarre's research at the Oceanographic Institute, which is why he spends these fifty-hour shifts on Sakonnet Island. That's where the Harbor Authority comes in. The narrows leading to the nesting grounds are far too unpredictable for an amateur pilot, so my job is to ferry the Catalan phocidologist across the bay on Tuesday mornings and to pick him up again on Thursday afternoons. Wally complains this is a waste of the taxpayers' money, but I think it's quite exciting. It makes me feel like I'm a part of science—a part of progress.

This is the sixth and final week of Dr. Navarre's study: the sort of bright, billowy day that makes me glad to work on the water. Soon the mist will burn off the shallows, leaving the low-hanging branches to the kingfishers, and legions of fiddler crabs will forage the mudflats for algae. I control the wheel with one hand and sip hot cocoa from my thermos while my passenger teaches his daughter the difference between fact and opinion. "The sky is *blue*. That's a fact," he says. "The sky is *beautiful*. That's an opinion. Because *I* think the sky is beautiful, that doesn't mean *you* have to."

The girl furrows her tiny brow. "You love me, don't you?" she asks.

Victor Navarre draws back her auburn bangs and kisses her on the forehead. "Of course, I love you. More than all the fish in the sea."

Patagonia bites her lower lip. "Is that a fact or an opinion?"

"That's a fact," he answers, unfazed. "Your Daddy loves you more than all the fish in the sea, and all the birds in the air, and all the stars in the sky."

I can't help thinking that if I ever did have children, I'd want their father to be as patient and as emotionally generous as this soft-spoken biologist. So maybe it's best that Wally doesn't want kids. Because my husband is bright and ambitious and dependable—you can't run your own small business very long if you're not—but he'd steer his offspring as far away as possible from whatever magic remains in the universe. "The last thing this family needs is another dreamer," I can hear him saying. "Trust me on this one, Penny. I come from a long line of dreamers who dreamed themselves straight out of the third largest whaling fortune in New England." That's why he doesn't want children—at least not yet—which, at my age, means never. Because he resents his own parents for bringing him into the world with so little. But Wally has a good heart. It's hard to blame him for being who he is, when you consider where he's come from.

"It's so kind of you to let Patagonia hitch along like this," says Victor Navarre. I've been warned that his daughter is always Patagonia, never Patty. "Are you sure you can handle her alone on the way back?"

Patagonia will not be staying at the field station. The plan is for me to return the girl to the pier, where Navarre's ex-wife will pick her up.

"We're going to have lots of fun," I say. "Aren't we, Patagonia?"

The girl has draped her arms over the starboard railing, letting the surf fleck dark droplets onto the sleeve of her windbreaker. She looks me over intensely and asks, "Are there boy-seals and girl-seals?"

"Another triumph for scientific inquiry," says Victor, grinning. "I can't imagine that I asked these sort of things when I was seven."

"When I was seven," I answer, "I wanted to study chimps. Like Jane Goodall."

Maybe I've said too much. Victor Navarre looks at me, puzzled—as though he's seeing me for the first time. It has probably never crossed his mind that I might be doing something other than ferrying him across Narragansett Bay. The truth is that I do enjoy my work with the Harbor Authority—I'm grateful not to be stuck behind the counter at the tackle shop like Wally, ladling out spearing by the ounce and running credit cards for kayak rentals—but while I like my work, I don't love it. I always expected I'd have more at thirty-six than a steady job and a pension fund. I don't even have a college diploma. So would I trade places with Victor Navarre? In a hummingbird's heartbeat.

"Primatology *is* interesting work. Important work," says Navarre. "If you're still interested in pursuing it, I could put you in touch with people."

"Thanks, but not this time around," I answer, trying to appear cheerful. "There's more than enough monkey business for me here on the bay."

That's when the girl shouts, "Seals!"

She's pointing east of the Usher Point Lighthouse, out into the shipping lanes.

"Dammit. I think she's right," I say. "They're moving."

"Those aren't seals," says Navarre. "Those are *whales*. Humpbacks. You've got a mother-calf dyad up front and a male escort following."

. . . . .

We've had a pod of minke whales frequenting the open channel for several summers now, and an injured right whale drew crowds to Newport last October, but this is the first time I've ever seen whales so far up the bay. The waters north of Goat Island aren't particularly hospitable to wildlife—it's hard to imagine what would lure these creatures under the Tottingham drawbridge and toward a busy estuary lined with loading docks and chemical drums. I'm particularly worried about the calf, who appears to be flailing against the current. The cow circles alongside him, the pair charting an uncertain course toward the mouth of the Bristol River. The bull, presumably the father, keeps his distance. When he's abreast of a gravel-laden barge, he breaches in a cloud of spray.

"That flailing is a normal feeding pattern," Dr. Navarre assures me. "They slap their flippers in order to startle fish. What concerns me more is that the mother *isn't* feeding—that she's letting the calf set their route."

"I'd better radio HQ," I say. "Whales are above my pay grade."

Dr. Navarre examines the animals through his binoculars. "Those whales are in trouble," he says. "We'd better phone the hotline up in Falmouth. I'll see if I can make out a tail print on the male."

I'm impressed by Navarre's calm—how easily he takes command of this unforeseen crisis. His expertise on whales, which

becomes apparent as he describes our trio's markings to the humpback tracker on Cape Cod, is downright encyclopedic. If I were
ever a disoriented sea mammal, this man is exactly the sort of
human being I'd want to have orchestrating my rescue.

"They're going to send a team out immediately," he says to me,
"but it's going to take them a couple of hours to get down here."

"Are the whales going to die?" asks Patagonia.

"I don't think so," says her father. "I hope not."

"I hope not too," says the girl. "Then I would cry."

Victor Navarre slides his cell phone back into the pocket of his
jeans. "I suppose we should follow them," he says. "Can we do that?"

The answer I've been trained to give is NO. We *can't* do that. I'll
get into beehives of trouble—maybe even an official reprimand—
for taking the patrol boat beyond the mouth of the Bristol. It's
been years since they've dredged the lower section of the river, or
charted its clearance, so Lord-only-knows what's projecting up
from the depths, just waiting to take a jab at my hull. Besides, the
Bristol runs through Massachusetts, outside the Harbor Authority's jurisdiction. On the other hand, that calf might be the most
adorable thing I've ever laid eyes on. It's poking its head out of the
water now—Navarre calls this "lunging"—and its big black eyes
and broad smile make it look like a human child. Almost. I'll also
admit that I'm enjoying my time with Dr. Navarre and his daughter, that I don't want this morning to end.

"We've got about five feet of hull draft," I say. "We should be
able to make it a few miles upstream without much trouble."

So we set out on our ad-hoc whale-tracking expedition—the
adventure I realize I've been dreaming of ever since this square-
jawed researcher with his creamy olive skin first stepped foot
over my gunwales. The tide is flowing in quickly, which should
give both the humpbacks and the S. S. Lovecraft some leeway to

maneuver. We pass beneath the interstate highway through a strait
that can't be more than eighty yards wide. Upscale homes mottle
the near bank, private pleasure boats docked at their backyard jet-
ties. On the opposite shore, Providence Power's massive hydroelec-
tric plant discharges plumes of angry steam into the cloudless sky.
Overhead, herring gulls drift on the spring breeze. Victor Navarre
opens his pack and retrieves a zip-lock bag full of sandwiches. All
peanut butter and jelly. He passes one to his daughter and another
to me. There are also pears, bananas, tangerines. A box of cold
pop-tarts for dessert. It strikes me that since the Lovecraft is one of
the new, toilet-and-faucet-equipped skiffs—eight identical vessels
named after supposedly famous Rhode Islanders—we could, in
theory, stay out here on the river until our food supplies run dry.

Navarre escorts his daughter to the toilet and shows her how it
functions. While he waits outside the door, he glances at his watch.
"My ex-wife is going to strangle me."

"Do you want to call her?"

"She's afraid to carry a cell phone." He rolls his eyes. "Brain
tumors."

That's when I remember I'm late for lunch with Wally. We're
supposed to meet at the Happy Clam on my break to go over the
rental agreement for his third shop. My husband is hoping to do
for tackle rental what Blockbuster did for videos. He's going to go
through the roof if I stand him up, but I'm reluctant to call him.
I'm afraid he'll convince me to cut short my whale watch.

"Is your ex-wife American?" I ask Navarre.

He nods. "We've been divorced over a year and it's still strange
to think of her as my *ex*-wife. Very strange." He lowers his voice.
"We have an expression in Catalan: *És pitjor el remei que l'enfermetat.*
The remedy is worse than the disease. Sometimes it's difficult not
to think that about divorce. Especially when there's a child."

"We have the same expression in English," I say.

To me, my words sound trite. Even dismissive. Navarre doesn't notice.

"But Angela and I are like two different species. She comes from a family of shouters—and when I won't shout back, she just shouts louder," Navarre says, as much to himself as to me. He tosses cusps of tangerine rind into the muddy water and adds, "My ex-wife is a plankton botanist," as though this explains her behavior.

Wally is also a shouter. I've never thought of him in those terms before, but he is.

"The one fact about whale behavior I remember from graduate school," says Navarre, "is that whale calves appear to grieve their parents just like humans. If a whale calf loses a father, it can descend into a terrible depression."

That's one of the saddest things I've ever heard. So I say as much.

"But it turns out that fathers are far more expendable than mothers," adds Navarre. "Most calves who lose their mothers are dead within weeks."

The toilet flushes inside the head and Patagonia reappears.

"What were you talking about?" she demands.

"About the whales," says Navarre. "About how we want them to turn around and go back to the ocean where they belong."

I take a look at the gauges. We're already six miles inland.

"They'd better turn around soon," I say. "They're going to run out of water."

. . . . .

The Cetology Research Laboratory in Falmouth phones back in less than an hour with a positive ID on the whales. The mother is Dandelion—half of a rare set of twins. Her nine-month-old calf is Excelsior. Interestingly, the male escort, Cornelius, is not the baby's

father, but a surrogate who has tagged onto the dyad. "The biological father died last March in a trawler collision off the coast of
Iceland," Navarre explains. I'm awestruck by the level of personal
history that is available on these animals. My own family—Yankee-
German-Irish firefighters and customs clerks and merchant seamen
from the Port Edward area—can't have left behind such a record.

"The good news is that this pair has gotten lost before, but
somehow they always manage to get reoriented," says Dr. Navarre.
"The bad news is that our rescue team is going to be delayed.
They've had another humpback sighting up near Gloucester, and
their helicopter is already out."

Patagonia tugs at her father's belt loop. Once again, she asks,
"Are the whales going to die?"

"I honestly don't know, honey," says Navarre. "I don't want
them to."

The girl turns to me. "My grandma died," she says. "That made
me cry."

I fight the urge to envelop the child in my arms and squeeze
tight. She's smiling at me—long recovered from her lost grandmother—but my eyes are tearing up.

"If we believe the whales are in any imminent danger, they want
us to pull in front of them and try to head them off," says Navarre,
as though this is an everyday feat. "Humpbacks avoid sound. They
apparently have fragile eardrums. If we make enough noise, we
might just divert them."

For some reason, I think of my passenger's ex-wife and her shouting. I can envision her rattling the delicate bones of his inner ears, the
miniature skeletal apparatus that so fascinated me in grade school.

"I'm not an expert," says Navarre. "But I don't think we should
wait for that rescue team from Falmouth. Do you feel up to some
whale diversion?"

"I'll give it a shot," I say, already accelerating. "Hold on tight."

The Lovecraft skims the water like a polished stone. Along the shoreline, children have gathered at the ends of docks to watch. Closer by, an elderly woman in a chartreuse sun visor waves to us from the deck of a luxury sloop. I'm about parallel with the mother and calf when my cell phone rings. I know it's Wally by the distinctive ring-tone: the Sailor's Hornpipe. As much as I don't want to, I flip open the lid.

I mouth the words, *my husband*, to Navarre. To my amazement, he winks at me.

I'm so dumbfounded, I let Wally repeat my name several times before I speak.

"Look, Wally," I say—not giving him a chance to unload, "I'm trying to rescue three lost whales and I can't talk right now. I'm really sorry about lunch. I'll call you when I get back to the marina."

And then I hang up. Just like that. And I shut off the phone.

If I stop to think, I'll feel guilty. So instead, I take us to full throttle.

Our patrol skiffs can hit about fifty knots in clear weather, and possibly even sixty with a strong enough tail wind, so it doesn't take more than about three minutes to cut in upstream of the humpbacks. Yet that's just a first salvo. The S. S. Lovecraft is only twenty-eight feet long. Nothing prevents the trio from swimming around us. I cut the engine and wait for Navarre's next command.

"Nice job," he says. "Okay, now it's time to shout."

A peculiar hush falls over the vessel, punctuated only by the wind-driven snap of the state flag above the cabin. Wally speaks a smattering of Portuguese—he checked traps for Cape Verdean lobstermen on weekends during high school—and now I finally understand how he feels when people ask him to "say something"; screaming on command is no easy task. It's not any easier surrounded by sun and waves and silence, when the entire world feels like an Impressionist seascape.

"GO AWAY!" Navarre hollers suddenly. "GO BACK DOWN RIVER!"

The naturalist stamps his feet, rocking the deck. He retrieves a frying pan from his pack and beats it with a wooden spoon. Then he climbs atop one of the bulkhead doors and extends a hand for me to join him. Soon, I'm standing beside him on the narrow elevated platform, our shoulders nearly touching. I take shallow breaths and keep my gaze focused on the water. Navarre returns to shouting and drumming.

"WE LOVE YOU," I yell at the whales. "WE DON'T WANT YOU HERE!"

"PATAGONIA," Navarre bellows. "DON'T YOU WANT TO SHOUT ANYTHING?"

The girl mulls over this invitation without making a sound, her hands plastered over her little mouth and fine beads of spume twinkling in her long auburn hair. I allow myself the unhealthy thought of pretending to be the child's stepmother—but only for a moment—because I realize this is a pipedream. What I *really* want, I suppose, is to keep my life with Wally, and *also* to have a life with Victor Navarre and his daughter. Not that that's actually going to happen. But even the thought of it makes me feel desperate. And guilty. I'd certainly make a better mother than plankton-mad Angela Navarre with her ferocious vocal cords and her brain tumor paranoia. As though to prove my point, Patagonia screams: "SHOUTING CAUSES CANCER! SHOUTING CAUSES CANCER!"

And then we are all belting out this same refrain: "SHOUTING CAUSES CANCER! SHOUTING CAUSES CANCER!"

We keep this up for what seems like hours, but is probably only a few minutes. At some point, I grin at Navarre. He grins back.

I can only wonder how we appear to the elderly woman on the nearby luxury sloop, whose husband has since joined her above deck. He's speaking into his cell phone. I suspect he's notifying the Massachusetts Harbor Guard. I try to imagine what he's saying: "Out here on the Bristol River there are two raving lunatics and a child taunting a trio of whales." I truly pity the unfortunate duty officer who has to respond to this call.

The whales themselves don't react to the clamor immediately. At first, Excelsior continues to slap-feed and Dandelion begins to blow like a living geyser, churning skyward ten feet of flume. Cornelius even swims toward us at one point, breaching only yards from the boat. He's between the Lovecraft and the dyad now—and I suddenly realize he's offering the mother and child protection, cover, like a father shielding his daughter from bullets. The baleen plates on either side of the bull's mouth look tense, as though he's in agony. I want to stop shouting, but deep down I know that his suffering is for the greater good. Soon, calf and cow lay still in the water—for a second, I fear they've fainted—and then they set off downriver. Cornelius breaches one final time, waving farewell with his broad tail, and follows.

All is still and quiet as marble. A breezy April afternoon.

Patagonia is the first to speak. "Did you save the whales?" she asks.

"*We all* saved the whales," answers Navarre. "*You* did amazing work."

"So they're not going to die?"

"It doesn't look like it," says her father.

"Good," says the girl. "Then I'm not going to cry."

"Nobody is going to do any crying," he agrees. "Do you know who else did amazing work? Captain Penny."

"Thank you," I say.

"I really mean that," says Navarre. "You're quite a woman."

I flash him an appreciative smile. Inside, I'm sobbing.

. . . . .

The mood on the S.S. Lovecraft is far more festive on the trip back down the Bristol. Now that Victor Navarre doesn't have to worry about the welfare of the humpbacks, he's free to enjoy them. And the animals truly are majestic! Mother and child perform intricate diving sequences, churning water over their backs. They vanish into the opaque water and erupt fifty yards away, projecting nearly their entire bodies airborne. It is quite a show. But, in my present state of mind, I'm unable to appreciate it. I recognize that this will be my last encounter ever with my passengers, certainly my last time with Patagonia. Most likely, my supervisor will ground my sea-feet while she prepares a report of this "misadventure" of mine. So if I don't say something to Victor now, I'll never have an opportunity.

The problem is I'm not that kind of woman. I'm just *not*. I took Wally for good and for bad—and I do love him. I like to tell myself that if I hadn't married him at nineteen, I would have finished at the state university, but that's a lie. The truth is that the daughters of Yankee-Irish-German harbor officers don't grow up to be field biologists. It's one of those immutable elements of reality. Nor do they throw away their husbands and pension plans for handsome Catalan phocidologists. But still . . . !

We trail the whales downstream, saying little. Patagonia stands on the far side of Victor, leaning against the railing. The girl looks sun-drenched and exhausted. Father and daughter are holding hands. She asks a question about how fast a person has to swim before she becomes a fish, and her father responds by explaining the differences between *degree* and *kind*. I take pleasure in listening.

Then—without warning—the girl folds her slender arms across her chest in displeasure. "We didn't see any seals," she exclaims. "All we saw were whales."

"That's true," concedes Navarre. "But the day isn't over yet."

It's *nearly* over, though. The humpbacks are approaching Goat Island. From there, it's only a few nautical miles to the open ocean. I'm seized with an impulse toward intimacy, a yearning to let my passenger know what I'm feeling.

"You're a very lucky man," I say to Victor.

"Yes, I am," he agrees, as if this is the most obvious fact in the world. "Are you sure you're not still interested in studying chimps? I really do know people."

I sense that this offer is neither idle nor selfless. That he's testing the waters.

"I don't know," I answer—honestly. "I don't even have a college degree."

"Jane Goodall didn't have a college degree when she first accompanied Louis Leakey to Africa," says Victor. "That didn't stop *her*."

I actually know this tidbit already. Yet I'm amazed that he does. Somehow, his knowing this obscure fact makes it okay when he claps his hand over mine on the railing. The three of us are now connected—hand to hand—like a family. The sun beats down upon us, warming my face. I close my eyes. I want to savor this moment, because I've wanted it for so long, but suddenly I'm thinking about the time Wally and I discovered an injured barn swallow on the steps behind the bungalow. About how he drove the animal to a special clinic and paid a week's worth of receipts for microsurgery on the bird's shattered wing, *because I wanted him to*—even though he'd been correct to think the efforts fruitless. That helpless swallow is what I'm thinking about while Victor Navarre gently kneads my knuckles.

"Are you happy, Penny?" Victor asks. "Like this?"

Am I happy? I'm not even sure what that question means any-more. I don't know how to reconcile how I feel now with how I felt holding Wally's hand at the pet cemetery while he said the Twenty-Third Psalm over the grave of a dead barn swallow. In any case, I don't have any opportunity to tell Victor what I'm feeling. Before I can open my mouth, Patagonia is shouting and pointing at the whales.

It's the mother. Dandelion. She's taken a sharp turn out of the channel and—as my eyes adjust to the bright daylight—I watch her pitch herself onto the sand bar on the leeward shore of Goat Island. The entire act takes only seconds, like a woman jumping from a bridge. One minute she's in the water, frolicking with her calf, and the next she's spread out like a hunk of meat under the hot afternoon sun. Seawater glistens off her enormous, twitching body. Cornelius remains in the channel, keeping a healthy distance between himself and the muddy reef. Closer by, the calf thrashes his dorsal fins as though beating his flanks in grief. I stand at the railing, speechless, waiting for Victor Navarre to issue the proper commands.

"Mother of God," he exclaims. "How do you like that?"

Navarre sounds calm, unruffled—as though he has the situation under control.

I'm not nearly so relaxed. "You've got to do something, Victor," I plead. "Please tell me what to do and I'll do it."

Victor Navarre just shakes his head grimly. "What can we pos-sibly do?"

"But what about the calf!" I scream. "What about the baby!"

Patagonia senses my alarm and starts sobbing gently. "I thought you promised the whales weren't going to die."

Her father places his hand on the back of her neck. "I didn't promise you that," he says. "I said I *hoped* they wouldn't die. But you don't need to be sad, darling. Death is an essential part of the natural world. Sometimes sick whales have to die so that newer, healthier whales can be born."

Victor Navarre says these words with such confidence, such conviction, that it's almost possible to believe that they're true.

"But what about the baby?" I say again. "The poor baby."

Victor places his hand on my shoulder to console me, but his touch is not one that can ease my grief. I am already thinking about what I will tell Wally of the day's turmoil and also about what I won't tell him—of the part of me that will come home to my husband for comfort and the part of me that will remain out there in the sand.

Live Shells

· · · · · · · · · · · · · · · · ·

I. The First Ex-Husband

Shelling picks up again in late autumn as the hurricane season gives way to the tourist onslaught and midwestern families strip-mine the beaches for whelks and murexes. Oversized out-of-state sedans clog the causeway, transforming Periwinkle Boulevard into a parking lot of exhaust fumes and churned-up dust, their horn-happy drivers drowning out the cries of the herring gulls and frightening the piping plover. Our running joke is that they're all interchangeable, these mainlanders, distinguished only by the color of their sun visors and the magnitude of their binoculars, but there's nothing funny about my first ex-husband passing himself off as a perfect stranger to my ninety-three year old grandmother. I find them one afternoon on the open-air porch sharing a pitcher of pink lemonade.

The decades are creased into Donald's face like the rings of a tree. He's grown a beard, put on weight, sprouted hair from the cusps of his ears. I approach unseen in the shade of a coconut palm and listen to his speculations on the recent cold snap and the prospects for the upstate orange crop while Grandmama nods and smiles and clicks her knitting needles together as though she's heard it all before. She was already an old woman when I married

Donald and she can no longer tell the difference between strangers and long-time acquaintances she's since forgotten, so she hedges her bets, treating even the water-meter man and the Jehovah's Witness proselytizers like kissing cousins. Donald is no exception. And me? I'm not sure how to proceed after twenty-one years, so I step into the afternoon sunlight, my jaw clenched to hold my composure, but at the very moment when Donald recognizes me, my eyes rivet to the double knot in the right sleeve of his shirt. My ex-husband's arm is missing at the shoulder. I stare at the haunting spot where the limb should be, unable to avert my gaze, fully conscious that I'm behaving the perfect fool.

"Hey pretty lady," he says through a self-satisfied grin. "Come here often?"

"What happened?" I ask.

I hurry forward, up the porch steps, until we're separated by only a body's length of plywood, then stop too quickly at the thought of a hug. Why am I concerned when I should be seething, hurling the insults I've hoarded since his departure? What right does Donald have to my pity? He seems to see clean through me, for his smile turns apologetic and he slaps his hidden stump with his remaining hand. "You mean this?" he says. "Gator took a piece off it. No big deal. What's an arm among friends?"

"My God, Donald," I gasp.

He responds with a laugh, a deep almost festive bellow from the core of his gut. "I knew that'd be your response, May," he says. "I actually crushed it on the job, at a machine tool shop in Dayton, Ohio. Sixteen years next month. Much less glamorous than a gator, but full workman's comp."

This is all *so* damn Donald—dropping in after two decades, joking about a missing limb—that I'm instantly on my guard. "What are you doing here?" I ask.

"You're still ravishing," answers Donald. "Eyes blue as the ocean. Do you remember when I'd say I could see all the way to Cuba just by looking into them?"

"What are you doing here?" I ask again, trying to add edge to my voice. I take a half step backward, resting my sandals on the porch rail, conscious that Grandmama has dropped her knitting into its basket to make room for higher drama. "I'm sorry about your arm," I add, "but I'm a busy woman."

"I should have written," replies Donald. "Don't think I don't know that, but the truth is I've been pretty busy myself. I did a couple of years for passing bad checks. Then I found God for a while, but I lost him again. The long and the short of it is that I've come back to say I'm sorry. So I'm saying it."

Donald finishes his canned speech and steps off the porch into the driveway where he digs his boot heels into the dust. I want to gouge his eyes out for showing up like this, for ruining my impending date, my first date in four months, but the bastard can tell his remarks about my eyes have hit home, that he'll get whatever it is he desires. He must know I've missed him all these years, on and off, through two bitter marriages and an autistic child and God knows how many nights alone with Mama and Grandmama. Now Mama is dead and Grandmama's eyes are swollen like apricot pits and the only good reason I can think of to hate him, this man who left me cold one night without a trace after six years sharing the same bed, is that he's been gone two decades and my life has changed so little in the interim that he still knows exactly where to find me.

"Apologize, my ass," I say. "What else?"

Donald lights a Pall Mall, tossing the match at the tail of an unsuspecting lizard, and I anticipate exactly what he is going to say before he says it. He's going to ask if I remember playing "lizard tails" in grammar school, how his pals collected the lopped tails by the hundreds and poured the full bucket into my gym locker. I'm caught off guard when, instead, Donald asks if I remember Andy Smithfield.

"I looked him up on the way down," says Donald, without waiting for a response. "He lives in Orlando. He's got six kids. I told them the story about how their dad ate a dozen lizard tails in the fifth grade and the boys loved it. They'd never heard it before."

"What else, Donald?"

"Lung cancer," he answers, taking a deep drag on his cigarette. "Metastasized. Three months, tops. So I thought I might crash here for a while and catch up on old times."

My ex-husband laughs again and I despise him for finding his own death so amusing. Grandmama laughs too, unsure of the joke but trying to please. Two anhingas settle on the low-hanging branches of a scrub oak where the waning sunlight glistens off their slick backs and I watch hypnotically as they yawn their wings in a display of collective indifference. They have no wisdom to offer.

"Don't worry," says Donald. "I'll pay rent."

His tone tells me that he knows I've already relented.

II. The Suitor

Tanner Colby, Crystal's special ed instructor, swings by at precisely seven o'clock with a dozen red roses tucked under one arm. He's sporting a three-piece white summer suit and a bola tie and he's slicked back his thick grey hair so that, although he's only forty-two, he resembles Ben Matlock on the television detective program. The little I know of Tanner bodes well: his sister died of Rett syndrome, he's a Mississippi transplant writing a biography of Anne Morrow Lindbergh in his spare time, the county recently honored him for excellence in teaching. Tanner couldn't make last month's open school night (he covers six mainland schools in addition to Cormorant Island) so we set up a private conference, then he dropped by my bookstore a couple of times, always on the pretext of being in the neighborhood although he lives sixty miles away, and one thing led to another until he practically apologized for asking me to dinner. He's phoned twice since to confirm that this is "officially" a date.

"Am I too early?" Tanner asks as I pass the flowers through the open door to my grandmother. "I'm supposed to be fashionably late, right, to show I'm not too interested?"

"You're too much," I answer. Then, fearing he may take this the wrong way, I add, "Perfect timing. I just put Crystal to sleep. It's only that I can't help wondering why a man like you would bring such lovely roses to a woman like me." I mean a thrice divorced woman of forty-eight whose ex-husband is napping on her fold-out sofa, but some things are best left unsaid.

We stroll arm in arm toward restaurant row, passing the Shellections Boutique, the Quartermast Tavern, the Tarpon Bay Motel where the cargo racks of the cars out front are loaded high with lawn chairs and water skis and fishing tackle. The dunes are visible through gaps in the undergrowth and the salt air carries the sounds of the sea—the rhythmic breaking of the surf, the rustle of the sand grass, the soulful pleas of mating spoonbills. These have been the limits of my world for nearly five decades and I can remember the first high-rises scaling the beachscape and the grizzled teams who constructed the causeway at a time when the tallest structure on the island was the ersatz windmill atop the Dairy Queen. Soon I'll be a life-longer, what we call a mollusk, because permanent inhabitants of Cormorant Island are allegedly as hard to break as the shells of a bivalve. Forty-eight years is nearly forever. To Grandmama, of course, that's nothing. On good days she remembers when the island was two islands, before the Hurricane of '26 choked the pass with silt. I'd like to share all this with Tanner Colby, to tell him how strange it is to have lived one's entire life in one place, not even a place of one's own choosing, but he'd probably take that for sour grapes or inertia, and I'm not sure it isn't, so I hold my tongue and let the sounds of night eclipse the sounds of day.

The tourists are lined out the door at the Admiral's Landing, but I throw a pleading glance at Doris behind the register and she ushers us to a window table. This is the top of the line for Cormorant dining (complimentary caviar appetizers, a smoked-fish bar, baby grouper served on fish-shaped plates) and I try to enjoy it, letting Tanner guide the conversation, feeling for him when he speaks of his dead sister and wipes his eyes with the cloth napkin. He's educated, earnest, maybe a bit too sincere for his own good, but if he loves me as much for Crystal as for myself, so much the better. I dread the moment when the key lime pie arrives and I must reveal the bombshell of the afternoon.

"My ex-husband showed up today," I blurt out during a conversational lull.

Tanner examines my words as though testing a fine wine. "I thought you had a restraining order," he finally says. "I can call my lawyer-friend in Tampa right after dinner."

"Not Peter," I explain. "Donald."

"Your first husband, right?"

"Right. He's terminally ill and he plans to use my place as a hospice."

"I see," Tanner says. His hands knot the corner of the tablecloth around his napkin ring and I'm afraid I've said something wrong. We sit in silence for several seconds, the din of the restaurant occasionally pierced by Doris's raspy voice calling numbers through the loud speakers. "I see," Tanner says again. "I'm sorry."

"Why are *you* sorry?"

"This is your way of telling me you're not interested, May, isn't it? It's okay. I just thought—you know—my sister and your daughter—well maybe—"

"But I *am* interested," I answer, much too loud, conscious that the elderly couple at the adjacent table has turned to stare at us. I lean forward and lower my voice. "It's not that at all," I say. "Trust me. My cards are on the table, Tanner Colby. I *am* interested. I only thought you might object to the situation and I can't turn Donald out. I just *can't*. He still gets to me, in spite of everything." I want to add, "And I'm still in love with him," but I know that will complicate matters and I'm not even sure if it's true.

Tanner smiles as though he's just recovered from a near-death experience and his hands start to tremble. I'm afraid he's going to burst into tears or shouts of jubilation.

"It gets worse," I say. "He asked me to invite you to dinner. Tomorrow night. I know that sounds ridiculous, my ex-husband inviting *you* to dinner at *my* house, but he has a way of doing these things. Of getting what he wants. When you meet him, you'll understand."

"It will be my privilege," says Tanner. "I never turn down the company of a beautiful woman, even if she is accompanied by a chaperon."

· · · · ·

Tanner walks me home through a warm wind. The moonlight distinguishes his profile, the strong jaw, the sharp nose, and although I'm too confused to be in the mood for anything, in fact I'm on the verge of a panic attack and I want nothing more than to sit on the deserted beach while I sort through the shambles of my life, I can't help hoping that he'll kiss me—even invite himself inside. I want a promise kiss, contract sex, something tangible to assure me that this man is as interested as he says he is. Instead he presses my fingers at the foot of the driveway and mutters that he knows I wouldn't want to kiss him on our first date. I'm too fatigued to disagree.

It's a good thing, too, because Donald is waiting for me on the porch, shucking a coconut with his pocket knife, playing emperor of the night to the swinging settee and the mangrove shadows. "I couldn't sleep," he says, "so I thought I'd stay up and meet the fellow."

Donald's voice oozes false-innocence, so much so that I'm tempted to claw my nails into the folds of flesh around his neck, but his face exposes his shame. He grins sheepishly, like a child who's recognized all along that he's doing something wrong and yet still can't resist the impulse. I feel my heart going out to him because he's lost an arm and because he's dying and, most of all, because if he weren't dying I might offer him the kiss I'd stolen from Tanner Colby and give him a chance to raise a daughter, to make up for lost decades. Only he *is* dying and neither Crystal nor I can afford another mistake.

"If you need an extra blanket," I say, "They're in the hall closet."

He doesn't call out my name until I've closed the screen door. His tone is tentative and I pretend not to hear him.

III. The Grandmother

I'm worthless at the bookstore the next morning but I can't afford to close early at the height of the tourist rush. We've been running in the red ever since Mama died and my night table is cluttered with the free clock radios First Florida doles out with business loans, so I flash a plaster smile at the clientele and gift-wrap mechanically, butchering my fingers, drifting into my own mental vacation. I should be contented; yesterday morning there were no men in my life, now there are two. Instead I feel my anger mounting at the last of the customers, resenting their leisure, their dalliance, their tourist ease, dreading the moment when they will abandon me to my impending dinner engagement. I wonder if the portly woman purchasing the gumbo and jambalaya cookbook has ever had to choose between the man she loves and the man who will take care of her. Or if the young mother browsing the kiddie corner feels trapped by her own children and hates herself for it. These thoughts get me nowhere, I know, so I am thankful (if surprised) when Grandmama appears at the end of the workday.

The mercury is in the high eighties, but my grandmother is bundled under a thick woolen sweater of her own design. The glow in her eyes relieves me, promises that nothing is amiss, suggests that she may even bear good news. She corrals me into the back room and surveys the stock shelves as though she's discovered a new planet.

"May," she says. "A word to the wise."

"It's Donald, right?"

"Such a gentleman," she says, "I think you should keep this one."

"Do you think so, Grandmama?"

This isn't my grandmother's first matrimonial endorsement, so I take her wisdom with a grain of salt. She'll say the same about Tanner. I'm about to thank her for her visit when the Suicide Point foghorn announces the close of the work day.

"Quitting time," I say, forgetting that Grandmama can't hear the low-pitched moan of the foghorn.

She scowls. "Mollusks never quit," she says. "They just..."

Her lips purse as she struggles for the close of the phrase, but she quickly forgets that she's lost her train of thought.

"I *do* like this one, this Donald," she says decisively. Then she rises on her tiptoes, leaning into my ear like a schoolgirl confessing a secret, and adds, "He reminds me of your first husband, only much, much older."

IV. The Family Dinner

Everything goes wrong from the outset. I've laid the diced carrots and cucumbers on the picnic table out back, started the swordfish patties on the charcoal grill, even lured Crystal to her favorite patio chair, when the thunderclouds roll in off the Gulf and checker the deck with thick, ominous droplets. The rain terrifies my daughter. She claps her hands over her ears and moans through her nose. Donald attempts to pacify her by taking her in his arms, which is the worst thing he can possibly do, so that by the time Tanner arrives, the food is ruined, our clothing is soaked through and everyone except for Grandmama is on edge. That's when we retreat to the dining room for makeshift television dinners and my ex-husband starts in about the live shells.

"Tanner," says Donald. "I can call you Tanner, can't I, seeing as how we're almost family? So Tanner, how do you feel about live shells?"

I know where this is going, but our guest doesn't, so he ponders the question while we listen to the sound of cutlery on porcelain. I've already sliced Crystal's roast beef into small squares and now I'm doing the same with Grandmama's, paring off the fat around the edges, hoping Tanner can hold his own until I re-enter the conversation. My grandmother won't mind if I take a break from her meat, but my daughter has a falcon's eye for consistency of detail; the rainstorm and two strange men have agitated her nerves enough for one evening, so I'm resolved to do the rest of the dinner by the book.

"Excuse me?" asks Tanner.

"I asked your feelings on live shells," Donald continues. "Do you keep them or do you throw them back?"

"I don't know," says Tanner. "I've never really thought about it."

"Well think about it," says Donald.

"Think about it," repeats Crystal. "Think, think about it."

This is a bad sign. She usually eats in silence and only speaks when she's upset. I serve my grandmother and slide back to my own seat, between Donald and Tanner, careful to walk the circumference of the table rather than behind my daughter's chair. The wind has picked up outside, whipping the palm fronds against the plate glass, raising the specter of another power failure. During the last major hurricane Crystal turned catatonic for three days and even if the lights only flicker, there's no telling how she'll take it, so I send up a prayer to the great god Florida Electric and pass my grandmother the rolls. Donald plucks a roll from the basket and bathes it in butter.

"Can you talk now?" Donald asks me.

I nod.

"I was just asking our friend Tanner about live shells. Do you remember how we used to fight about live shells, May?"

"How could I forget?"

"Think, think about it," says Crystal. "Live shells."

Donald lights a cigarette and pours Budweiser into a styrofoam cup for use as an ashtray. He offers his pack around, then deposits it before Tanner like a threat. "They're good for me," he says. "Once you have lung cancer, they can't do you any more harm. It's a great relief."

"I don't have lung cancer," answers Tanner, staring into his plate. I reach under the table and squeeze his hand. "I've thought about it," he says, "and I think it's only right to throw them back. Not that

I'm an expert, mind you, but it seems that you'd want the shells to grow to maximum capacity. On a one-time basis, you may lose, but if others also throw theirs back, then everybody comes out ahead."

This answer is too complex for Donald. "Sure, take her side," he says, pushing his plate toward the center of the table and opening his second beer. "I say finders, keepers. I say that about shells and I say that about women. Don't you agree with me, Tanner? You wouldn't throw a woman back, would you, even if it meant that everybody came out ahead?"

"Women aren't like shells, Donald," I say sharply. "Let's talk about something else. Tanner's from Mississippi, so he doesn't know about all this."

"There's only one way to learn," says Donald. "Say, have you told our friend here about how we used to go skinny-dipping at Suicide Point?"

"Think, think about it," says Crystal. "Live shells."

"Did you?" asks Tanner.

"I'm going to go down there next week to scatter Mama's ashes," I say to divert the conversation. "I keep putting it off because I want to take Crystal and I'm not sure if she can handle it."

"I'd be glad to come," offers Tanner, "if you think it will be easier for her."

That's a conversation stopper, for some reason, so we sit uncomfortably and listen to Grandmama's snores. She's dozed off again, which means it's bedtime for Crystal, but I'm afraid to leave my two men alone together. Donald's liable to pull one stunt or another, to pitch some deal where he gets me until he dies and then passes me off to Tanner, as though anyone other than my ex-husband could tolerate such an arrangement, let alone conjure it. What scares me is that the solution, though absurd, now seems perfectly plausible. I push my chair away from the table, thinking the time has come to bring our dinner party to an early close, when Donald restrains me with his arm.

"Let's *all* go to Suicide Point," he says. "We'll make it a family outing. Your grandmother, the girl, everybody."

"Really, Donald," I say, "This isn't a joking matter."

"I'm not joking. Tomorrow's Saturday. We'll head out at dawn, scatter the ashes, make a day of it. No skinny-dipping, I promise. Let's see what our friend Tanner here thinks of that."

Tanner looks to me for guidance, but I have none to offer. I can't risk an argument in front of Crystal and on the surface there's nothing remarkably unreasonable about Donald's suggestion, except that it's bound to lead to more trouble. I threaten Donald with my coldest stare, but he just laughs.

"What do you say, Tanner?" he persists. "A family outing?"

"I don't know," says Tanner.

"Well I do," answers Donald. "It'll be fun. I always liked May's mother. It's too bad you never had a chance to meet her."

I could kill him for this, I *should* kill him, but then it strikes me that he'll be dead in three months anyway and that's the most awful thought I can imagine. All I can do is retrieve Tanner's umbrella from the bathtub and escort him to the door, taking pains not to let Crystal hear the screen creak. When I return, she and Donald are engaged in a warped conversation, repeating the phrase, "Think, think about it," to each other like two stubborn children resolved to have the last word.

V. The Excursion to Suicide Point

Tanner yields to my ex-husband in every aspect of the trip, letting him pay for the rental boat, even indulging his need to sit at the prow. The seating arrangement is particularly awkward, as Donald can only maneuver one oar, but he insists on rowing while

Tanner sits on the ice cooler and braces the urn with Mama's ashes between his legs. This will slow our progress somewhat, making the journey easier on Grandmama and Crystal, but Tanner's pride has clearly been wounded. He sulks under his safari hat and makes no effort to help Donald release the moorings. I watch my ex-husband unwind the coil with one arm and I'm willing to play along with his twisted idea of machismo until he braces the tow-line between his teeth and retrieves a bolt-action rifle from his duffle bag. This is too much, even for me.

"Enough, Donald," I say. "You've gone too far."

Donald removes the tow-line from his mouth without relinquishing the rifle. "You don't like it, May? It's a Schmidt-Rubin. Imported from Switzerland. It'll come in handy if we startle a gator."

"Check it at the marina," I say. "Somebody is liable to get hurt."

My ex-husband steps forward, sending a shudder through our little vessel, and settles into the bow. The tow-line pulls taut in his grip. If I'm going to object to the gun, this will be my last opportunity. I glance at Tanner, hoping he will join me, but he's too busy fuming over past slights. Maybe he knows when to quit. Crystal is on the floor of the boat, perched between the two metal seats, seemingly soothed by the ripple of the waves. My grandmother has already propped herself on a sponge cushion and dozed into her morning siesta.

"Dammit, Donald," I say, careful not to raise my voice, "either you leave that awful thing somewhere or I'm getting out of this boat."

"What are you afraid of May?" he asks. "You're not afraid that I'm going to shoot someone, are you? That we're going to return with one less passenger?"

"Of course not," I say, knowing that my fears are groundless, trying to convince myself that I'm being irrational and Donald means no harm. He has a point too. I'm not actually afraid that he'll shoot anyone, only angered by his petty attempts at one-upmanship. "You can't bring it though," I add. "Suicide Point's on a nature preserve. They'll fine you."

Donald bellows and releases the tow-line. "I'll pay the fine in three months," he says, "They can take it out of my vast estate." He rests the rifle against the gunwale, picks up an oar, then reconsiders and extends the weapon in my direction. "I'll make you a deal," he says. "Our friend Tanner can hold onto this, if he swears not to shoot me. How does that sound?"

This is Donald's way of burying the hatchet, of admitting he's wrong *without* actually admitting he's wrong, so I take the gun and pass it back to Tanner. He accepts it stoically and slides in under his seat. Then he removes his safari hat, wipes the sweat from his brow with the back of his sleeve, and uses the hat to shield his lips from Donald while he mouths the words, "I love you." I force a smile. We haven't even left the marina and I can already tell this excursion has been a grave mistake.

Silence ensues as we ease our way between the sandbars, following the Park Service buoys to the mouth of the swamp. The trip to Suicide Point is only three miles as the crow flies, but it's a good hour's journey through narrow, winding channels of mangrove. Alligators sun themselves in the shallow water; great blue herons and cattle egrets trawl the tidal pools; terns circle overhead and dive for distant prey. This is the Cormorant Island the tourists crave, the pristine habitats which could complete their bird lists and fill their roles of film, but it's rare for them to venture past the visitors center and its adjoining boardwalks. Only locals brave the back country. We glide past several confirmed "mollusks" fishing from a power boat, identities confirmed by their polite nods and absolute silence, then coast around the leeward side of Dead Man's Neck and emerge onto the open salt-marsh that leads to our destination.

The view is breathtaking, though I have seen it countless times: Thousands of shorebirds basking on the sand flats, savoring the vestiges of the night's cool breeze. Soon the sun will burn off the last of the early morning mist and they will flee to the shadows of the mangroves. I haven't experienced this awe since my last voyage to Suicide Point and I suddenly understand that this is part of Donald's game, that somehow *he knows* I haven't been back here without him. My stomach muscles flutter uneasily as I fold my arms across my chest.

"How does our friend Tanner like this?" Donald asks, his voice drawing me back to the present. "It's a once in a lifetime view, don't you think?"

"Pretty impressive," agrees Tanner. "I wish I knew the different species of birds."

"You would wish that," says Donald. He drops his oars and stretches his arm, letting the current pull us onto the far bank. "You're now resting on Suicide Point," he says. "Do you know where they got the name Suicide Point? They say that once you've seen this view, there's nothing else worth living for."

My ex-husband steps out of the boat and waits for us to follow; then he secures the tow-line to a mangrove root. Grandmama leads Crystal by the hand and I'm surprised how well my daughter's handled the journey, that's she's managed the entire hour without so much as a moan or a repetition. Only when Tanner hands me the urn with my mother's ashes and I hold it out toward Crystal, hoping that somehow she'll connect with this moment, do I notice that her lips have worked themselves into a frenzy. She's mouthing the words, "I love you, I love you," as though her existence depended upon it.

Donald steps up beside me, his stump only inches from my shoulder, his gaze fixed on Crystal's mouth. It takes him several seconds to decipher her pantomime, but when he does, he says, "You're not the only one, kiddo," and, reaching across his body, draws me toward him with his arm. I know what is going to happen, but I don't have time to push Donald away. Crystal clasps her hands over her ears, opens her mouth wide, and produces a high-pitched clicking sound by beating her tongue against her palate. A similar episode preceded her catatonic spell.

"Please, Donald," I say, wresting myself from his grasp. "Not here. Please."

Tanner's voice echoes mine. "Not here," he says, his voice cold and firm. "You're upsetting the child."

"Mind your own business," says Donald. Then, "I didn't mean any harm."

"The child's business is my business," answers Tanner. "You can make an ass of yourself if you want to, you can even make an ass of me, but you have no business scaring that girl. Do I make myself clear?"

I know ahead of time that Tanner's warning, like Donald's pass, will have instant repercussions and I clutch the urn to my bosom in a burst of momentary panic before charging toward Crystal to shield her eyes from what I fear may be the worst. One of my sandals catches on a mangrove root, tumbling me head first into the wet sand. I am grateful that I've kept hold of the urn, that my daughter's clicking has suddenly softened into a melancholy whir. Only my grandmother's hoarse shriek alerts me to the disaster unfolding behind my back: My ex-husband is swinging at Tanner with a muddy oar.

The two men are facing each other several yards up the sand, squaring off like professional fighters, the underdog wielding a weapon to even the odds. Donald lunges suddenly, using the oar as a dagger, but the blow glances and they roll to the earth in an explosion of wet sand while Crystal's whirring drowns out their curses.

"Stop!" I shout. "For God's sake, Donald! Stop!"

He ignores me and I can see that he's wrapped his arm around Tanner's throat, that he's slowly crushing his windpipe. Tanner has his own arms clasped around Donald's back, the nails digging into the flesh at the base of his skull. They roll over, once, twice, locked together like the halves of a clam. I propel myself toward the boat and grab hold of the rifle.

"Stop it, Donald!" I scream. "Stop or I'll shoot you, so help me God!"

The top-most body instantly tenses and my ex-husband cranes his neck, straining to find me with his eyes. When he sees me, he releases his hold completely, letting Tanner regain his breath, and pushes himself to his knees. His breath is hard. Shell fragments mat his hair and beard. I step toward him.

"I'm sorry, May," he says. "I just got carried away."

"Put your arm up!" I order.

"It's all right, May," he says. "It's over. All out of my system."

"Put your arm up!" I shout again.

Donald grins suddenly. "You wouldn't shoot a one-armed man," he asks, "Would you?"

"Not one more word," I threaten.

I take another step forward and he slowly raises his arm above his head. His eyes dart across the sand flat, searching for an escape, but the realization that it's just him and me wipes the last traces of a smile from his lips. My ex-husband's arm starts to tremble and I can see the fear panning across his face, the creases tightening, his lips starting to quiver as he comes to terms with the seriousness of his predicament. If he'd only fought for me two decades earlier, none of this would have been necessary, but now I'm relishing every moment of his fear, prolonging each second of uncertainty, letting him anticipate the shot. How can he possibly know that I won't shoot him? How can he possibly know that he's now the man I've been waiting for all of my life?

Jacob M. Appel is a physician, attorney and bioethicist based in New York City. He is the author of more than two hundred published short stories and is a past winner of the Boston Review Short Fiction Competition, the William Faulkner-William Wisdom Award for the Short Story, the Dana Award, the Arts & Letters Prize for Fiction, the *North American Review*'s Kurt Vonnegut Prize, the *Missouri Review*'s Editor's Prize, the *Sycamore Review*'s Wabash Prize, the *Briar Cliff Review*'s Short Fiction Prize, the H. E. Francis Prize, the New Millennium Writings Fiction Award in four different years, an Elizabeth George Fellowship and a Sherwood Anderson Foundation Writers Grant. His stories have been short-listed for the O. Henry Award, *Best American Short Stories*, *Best American Nonrequired Reading*, *Best American Mystery Stories*, and the Pushcart Prize anthology on numerous occasions. His first novel, *The Man Who Wouldn't Stand Up*, won the Dundee International Book Prize in 2012. Jacob holds graduate degrees from Brown University, Columbia University's College of Physicians and Surgeons, Harvard Law School, New York University's MFA program in fiction and Albany Medical College's Alden March Institute of Bioethics. He taught for many years at Brown University and currently teaches at the Gotham Writers' Workshop and the Mount Sinai School of Medicine.